BOMB CYCLONE

BOMB CYCLONE

J.A. ADAMS

A NOVEL

atmosphere press

Published by Atmosphere Press

Cover design by Matthew Fielder

atmospherepress.com

For my husband, Joseph; my son, Matthew;
my brother, John; and in memory of my son, John

BRIEFING

In 1922, the Soviet Union was formed following a treaty signed by the Republics of Armenia, Azerbaijan, Georgia, Belarus, and Ukraine. By the 1980s, there were fifteen Soviet Socialist Republics. Originally led by Lenin, Stalin took over in 1924 until his death in 1953. Those who disagreed with Stalin's totalitarian rule were sent to gulags, cruel labor camps whose numbers of prisoners grew to millions over the course of his dictatorship.

But the USSR was on its slow course to destruction. By 1985, Gorbachev's reign saw him move the USSR from Marxist-Leninism toward social democracy, permitting elections and a multi-party system. But his looser economic and political policies, perestroika and glasnost, along with severe corruption and a failing economy, destabilized Soviet control and led to the dissolution of the Soviet Union in 1991.

After the fall, Ukraine finally escaped Russia's iron-fisted control but was one of the poorest republics of the former Soviet Union. With corrupt leaders during its nascent democracy-building, Ukraine's GDP fell by half between 1991 and 1994. Its iron and steel mills were collapsing until Russian oligarchs took them over. The oligarchs saved many Ukrainians their jobs, but at what cost? Oligarchs made vast sums while Ukrainians remained poor.

Nearly everyone in Ukraine spoke both Russian and Ukrainian. In eastern Ukraine, in the Donbas region of Donetsk and Luhansk, many Russian-speaking Ukrainians were separatists who aspired to reunite with Russia.

In 2004, authorities rigged the presidential election to elect Russia's choice, Yanukovych, president of Ukraine. The Orange Revolution protesting the corrupt election ensued, and a new election was ordered by Ukraine's Supreme Court. This time, Ukraine's choice, Yushchenko, won and served until 2010.

In 2010, Yanukovych, having been groomed by Paul Manafort, won the presidential election. He proved to be a puppet of Russia, breaking his promise to move toward agreements with Europe as he had promised in his campaign. His false promises led to the bloody Euromaidan demonstrations in Maidan Square in Kyiv, also known as the Revolution of Dignity, and culminated in his being ousted in 2014, after which he and his administration fled to Russia with millions from the Ukrainian coffers, where he remains in exile.

2014 was also the year Russia annexed Crimea from Ukraine, a move that has never been recognized by the UN or the international community. Pro-Russian separatists, along with unmarked Russian soldiers, demonstrated in favor of unity with Russia. These Russian-backed separatist militias have been fighting the Ukrainian resistance for nine years.

CHAPTER 1

DECEMBER 1994

How could anyone lose a nuke? Difficult as it may sound, Ukraine, with a little help from Mother Nature, accomplished just that. Three years after the Soviet Union's fall, Ukraine, holding a third of the Soviet nuclear arsenal, agreed to return all the nukes to Russia and destroy all their silos. Within the agreement were also assurances that Ukraine would maintain political independence from Russia and respect for its borders. Had Ukraine not agreed, they would have faced threats from Russia as well as from the U.S. and NATO allies. Under some pressure, Ukraine signed the Budapest Memorandum in 1994, the nuclear non-proliferation treaty, along with the U.S., Russia, and Britain. Ukrainians have long questioned the expedience of that decision. But what was done was done.

Some of the nukes were transferred to Russia via the Black Sea Fleet, the Soviet fleet that Presidents Yeltsin of Russia and President Kravchuk of Ukraine had divided between Russia and Ukraine in 1992, shortly after the

Soviet breakup. Twenty percent of the sailors took an oath of allegiance to Ukraine, Senior Lieutenant Bronislav Kravchenkos among them.

Soon after the partial transfer of nukes, reports arose that several nuclear weapons had disappeared, ripped from the ship by a sudden violent bomb cyclone out of North Africa. During investigations of the loss, the commission in charge of the search went silent, which had the desired effect, eventually, of a general amnesia among the population on both sides of the Atlantic. But according to Bronislav, neither the Russian nor the Ukrainian militaries suffered from that amnesia.

Nor did young Mykola Kravchenkos, Bronislav's son, suffer from the general amnesia. He had overheard a few parts of the story from his father and his father's comrade, Lieutenant Balanchuk, both of whom had been on a small artillery ship based in Sevastopol, Crimea, tasked with transferring some of the smaller nukes from Ukraine to Russia.

Disillusioned by escalating Russian hostilities, Ukrainian corruption, and a failed economy, Bronislav decided to retire from the Ukrainian navy as soon as he became eligible and emigrate with his family to the U.S., along with thousands of other Ukrainian émigrés who scattered to various locales, including Russia and the West.

Bronislav's navy comrade, Volodymyr Balanchuk, had retired earlier and immediately moved to the U.S., where his family settled in New Kensington, Pennsylvania, a small suburb of Pittsburgh. Naturally, Bronislav called him for advice about making a move.

"Why don't you come to New Ken, as the locals call it?" Volodymyr said, excited at the prospect of seeing his old comrade. "Several Ukrainian families have settled in the area, so we've made friends to play card games like Durak and share Stoli with us."

"We also like to play cards. And to drink a little vodka, of course!"

"Yah! Always a little vodka, or maybe some cognac, eh, Bronislav? Good food, good cognac, good friends. What's not to like? You must come."

"Sounds tempting, Volodymyr. But what about jobs, my friend? I have to work, you know."

"Of course! There's work here at PPG, just four miles away in Springdale. I work there, and you could go right to work too. Pay's good if you don't mind some overtime. Beats working for the oligarchs."

"You make it sound inviting, Volodymyr. But my English is not so good as yours."

"Don't worry. We all translate for each other in the mills. I'll put in a good word for you and maybe we can work side by side, so I can help you. They're hiring Ukrainian immigrants now since the Soviet breakup. You won't be sorry, Bronislav."

"It sounds tempting. But how are house prices there? I'm not a rich man."

"Nor are we. Houses here are cheaper than you might think. The U.S. is recovering from a recession, and housing prices have stayed low. If you sell your house in Sevastopol, you'll have a good down payment."

"You drive a hard bargain, Volodymyr. It's a scary move, all the way to America. But we've got to go someplace. Of course, having good friends in the U.S. already is certainly a plus. Let me talk to Aneta and see if she agrees. She and Daryna are good friends, and she'll like the idea of having friends nearby."

"Tell her Daryna's church is close by, too, the Holy Virgin Ukrainian Orthodox Church. I know Aneta likes to get involved in her church. And your family is welcome to stay with us until you can find your own place. We Ukrainians need to stick together. It would be great to catch up and tell Navy lies, no? Remember when our Artemas got diphtheria in '91? I was on a mission in the Black Sea then, and you came to my wife's rescue. We'll never be able to repay you, Bronislav."

"Oh, Volodymyr, you'd gladly have done the same for me."

That evening, Bronislav and his wife Aneta went online to look over available homes in New Kensington, Pennsylvania. "It looks like a nice town," Aneta said, "but such a huge expense to move to the United States."

"The good thing is our home here should sell quickly," he assured her. "Plus, we'll be moving into a small town with several Ukrainian families nearby. We'll stay with Volodymyr and Daryna at first, so Daryna can help you adjust."

"I suppose you're right. I won't feel so homesick since we have friends there. Oh, the boxes we'll need! The packing! How will we ship all our things?"

"Don't worry about all that now. We'll get it all done, and I believe the U.S. will be a much better place to raise our children."

"Of course, you're right, love. You're always right." She left the room, muttering to herself about all the work and expense of moving.

⅄

The next day, Bronislav called Volodymyr. "Well, old pal, we've decided to take you up on your generous offer, if you're sure you and Daryna don't mind putting us up for a while. That'll give us time to become familiar with the area, and Aneta said she'll feel much better with Daryna to help her acclimate. Aneta wants to find just the right house with just the right kitchen, of course."

"Ah yes, the Ukrainian woman and her kitchen. I understand completely. And Daryna will enjoy having Aneta here."

And so it was settled. The Balanchuk children, Artemas and Galyna, would be heading back to the University of Pittsburgh in January, so the Kravchenkos would stay in their two bedrooms, one for Aneta and Mykola's sister, Anya, and the other for Bronislav and Mykola.

After completing all the government's red tape, it didn't take long for Bronislav to sell their modest home in Sevastopol, the beautiful port city in Crimea on the Black Sea, where he'd been stationed. Volodymyr Balanchuk found an American sponsor for Bronislav's immigration visa, and the Kravenchokos embarked on the long, tedious voyage to the U.S.

With Volodymyr's help, Bronislav easily landed a job at PPG Industries as Volodymyr's apprentice for six months. Soon Aneta located a modest bungalow just down the street from the Balanchuks, with "just the right kitchen." The whole family approved of her choice, and by the beginning of 1995, they had settled into their "new to them" home in their "new to them" country. Bronislav worked alongside Volodymyr at PPG, so language wasn't a problem, and Bronislav was a quick study. The Kravchenkos and Balanchuks remained close friends, visiting each other for drinks, dinner, and Durak nearly every Saturday night. Bronislav never forgot his debt to Volodymyr Balanchuk.

Mykola was seventeen at the time, a senior at Valley High in New Ken. His sister, Anya, was fifteen. Like other young Ukrainians, Mykola and Anya had studied English in Ukraine, so they were able to catch up quickly in their new school.

A personable and handsome young man with a wide, sincere smile, wavy black hair, fair skin, and translucent blue eyes, Mykola was popular among Valley's students, especially the girls, who began affectionately calling him Mickey. The school served American and some Ukrainian students, so there was competition for "the new boy" and his attention among those two groups.

"Mickey, please come to a party Saturday at my house. My parents will be away," Marie entreated with a sly wink.

"Hey, Mickey," Tatayana followed, "I'm having a little party at my house on Saturday. We have vodka."

While the girls glared daggers at each other across the hall, Mykola, not wanting to insult either girl, simply answered, "I'm sorry, but I've already promised to attend a dinner party with my family at the Balanchuks' on Saturday. But thanks for asking."

The competition for his friendship made it virtually impossible for Mykola to establish lasting relationships. But no matter; as an expat, he continued to follow the latest news from back home, not allowing himself time for socializing. Mykola was a deep thinker who never lost his love and concern for Ukraine, as troubled as it was. He also listened anxiously to his father, who often discussed with Volodymyr the lost nuke and the danger it posed if the wrong people found it. One night when Bronislav saw Mykola listening to their conversation, he said, "Come over here, son. You remember when my crew was transporting the nuclear weapons through the Kerch Strait?"

"Of course, Tato. I remember." Mykola didn't reveal all that he had overheard.

"I think you're old enough to hear the whole story. Come and sit with Volodymyr and me, and I'll tell you about it."

Mykola found a seat on the couch next to his father.

"When that surprise bomb cyclone out of North Africa battered our ship with gale force winds, it tossed the crew around like toy soldiers. We grabbed for anything within reach. We were lucky our ship wasn't capsized. All of us could have drowned that night."

"Oh, Tato! I never realized it was that dangerous! Thank God you were OK. What would we have done without you?"

"Don't think of that now. We're safe here, son. Maybe I shouldn't tell you more."

"No, please. I need to learn the truth."

"OK, you're nearly a man now, old enough to know everything. Once through the strait, the storm blew our ship north and west. We finally made it to the north shore of Kerch Peninsula, slightly more protected from the gale force winds, where we ran ashore. The cyclone had ripped apart the cables lashing the suitcase nukes to the deck and rolled some of the bombs into the sea just north of the peninsula. You remember where we used to fish?"

"Of course, I remember. Tatarka Beach. I still miss our fishing trips with you and Vlad."

"I know you do, son. We all do. Anyway, most of the lost bombs were found, but one is still missing. The fuses have been removed, but now that the pro-Russian separatists hope to reunite with Russia, my fear is that they could find the bomb and make dirty bombs to use against our people. Some of our sailors were Russian sympathizers and moved to Russia, so they know the general area the bomb might be in, just as we do. I fear our country may be heading toward war."

"War!? Oh no, Tato."

"Not right away, Myko. But we must consider that possibility in the future. Russia is rattling its sabers, and I'm afraid the pro-Russian separatists are listening."

When Mykola was a child in Ukraine, his family had often vacationed on Kerch Peninsula, at the far eastern edge of Crimea, protruding into the Sea of Azov and forming the Kerch Strait. Mykola's fondest childhood memories were of family times at the beach, building sandcastles, swimming, and fishing in the sea with his father and Anya. Sometimes his best friend Vlad was allowed to come with them. Now, Myko dreamed of returning one day to search for the lost bomb. Of course, he didn't dare tell his father of his decision.

To call his dream an obsession might be a stretch, but he knew about the tensions within Ukraine and about the Russians and pro-Russian separatists who, his father and Volodymyr had said, were also interested in finding the bomb. Mykola tried to learn as much as he could about the tenuous independence of Ukraine, as well as the deepening tensions with Russia since the dissolution and the failing economy that had resulted in his family's emigration. Of course, he was too young now to attempt such a dangerous undertaking as finding the bomb, and he knew his father would never agree to it. He would have to plan on a trip as soon as he was old enough to support himself. Hopefully, it wouldn't be too late by then.

During this, his senior year at Valley High, Mykola worked hard and got accepted into Ohio State University, majoring in political science, an obvious choice considering his deep interest in politics and humanities in his homeland. He went on to earn a Master's and a Ph.D. in political science at the University of Michigan. Grad school dragged on, as it does, until finally, during his last semester of finalizing and defending his dissertation, which he named *Crisis in Ukraine: Putin's Obsession with Soviet Reunification*, and after three one-week-long interviews at colleges that showed an interest in him, Mykola was offered and accepted an assistant professorship in political science at Youngstown State University, a mid-sized university in Ohio, just over an hour from his family in the Pittsburgh suburb.

He wasn't in Youngstown long before he was beguiled

by Sarah Beekman, a professor of International Relations who introduced herself immediately to the handsome new PoliSci professor. Until now, his studies had been his first and only priority. Only now did he allow himself limited time for socializing, soon realizing how inexperienced and awkward he was at dating, especially dating an American with entirely different customs.

"Do you mean to tell me you've never even had a girlfriend?" Sarah asked incredulously on their first dinner date.

"Sarah, I've been so concerned with research, getting my degree, and becoming gainfully employed that I never had the time or inclination to meet someone. I have to say, I'm enjoying my first date immensely."

"But do you mean to tell me that you're a . . . VIRGIN?"

"Yes, I'm afraid so," he said, chuckling awkwardly. "Not scared off yet, I hope?"

"Well, it sounds like quite a challenge for some young lady. But, no, of course I'm not scared off."

After that awkward discussion, they moved to other topics and realized they might have a good deal in common.

Sarah told him, "I've also been teaching about the crisis in Ukraine in my International Relations class. Quite a few Ukrainian immigrants moved to Youngstown after World War II, and others joined families here after the Soviet dissolution. A few of my students are immigrants or descendants of immigrants. Naturally, they're concerned over current tensions in Ukraine. Some of them still have friends or grandparents there."

Having such a common interest, Mykola and Sarah discussed events in Ukraine long into many nights. Naturally, it didn't take long for Mykola to acclimate to not just having a friend but having a kindred spirit in his life. Their discussions contributed to their classroom teaching, and Mykola was quite taken with Sarah. Their relationship progressed naturally and rapidly from sharing meals and political discussions to sharing Mykola's apartment.

Mykola's career in teaching was perfectly suited to his interests, his love life was thriving, and the years seemed to fly by. He felt that he had finally found true contentment. But he'd had no news of the lost nuke, and the desire to find it still burned in his heart.

He only hoped Sarah would understand.

CHAPTER 2

ODESA, UKRAINE, 1994

In Odesa, Ukraine, considered by many the most beautiful city in Ukraine, Aleksander and Olga Kovalski welcomed their first and only child into the world on February 15, 1994, ten months before the dramatic Budapest Memorandum agreement with Russia, Britain, and the U.S. The magnificent blue-eyed baby girl arrived with hair so blonde it looked almost white. At the time, the Winter Olympic Games were being held in Lillehammer, Norway, and the world was being charmed by a 16-year-old female figure skater from Ukraine, Oksana Baiul.

Olga begged, “Please, Aleksander, let’s name our daughter after the Ukrainian skater. Our baby is so beautiful, just like Oksana Baiul.”

Aleksander, as infatuated with the young champion skater as everyone else in Ukraine, concurred heartily. “Yes, Olga. I think Oksana would be the perfect name for our little girl. Maybe she’ll even be a famous skater like her namesake, eh, Olga?”

"Oh, yes," said Olga, clapping her hands in delight. "We'll enroll her in classes when she's old enough. Maybe she'll grow up to be an Ice Angel."

Two months later, they christened their child Oksana Aleksandrovna Kovalska, with the Ukrainian feminine ending for Kovalski at the Orthodox Transfiguration Cathedral in Odesa.

Oksana amazed the Kovalskis. She walked at only eight months and already knew a few simple Russian words, the primary language of Odesa. The Kovalskis often took their toddler to watch ice skaters perform at the skating school, where she pretended she was also skating, twirling on tiptoes along the sidelines of the rink. They enrolled Oksana in a toddlers' class at age three, expecting wonderful things from her. The precocious child was ecstatic and said in her baby talk, "Tato, Mama, watch 'Sana spin!"

"She'll no doubt become an acclaimed skater," her teacher assured Olga. "She's one of the most graceful young girls we've seen on skates. We'd like her to come and practice at least two hours a day."

Oksana was proud of all the attention she was getting and followed the long practice schedule her teacher prescribed with never a complaint.

"Mama, watch my axel!" she hollered to Olga at age seven.

"Magnificent, Oksana!" Olga was proudly taking it all in from the sidelines, so thrilled with Oksana's progress that she spoke of little else. Friends were becoming tired of hearing about Olga's young prodigy daughter and had begun avoiding her at the market.

⅄

Sadly, Olga's dreams of Oksana becoming another "Ice Angel" were dashed when Oksana, at age nine, had a tragic fall while attempting a double axel and suffered a compound fracture of both the tibia and fibula. Her skating days were over, along with Olga's dream for her daughter's future. Olga and Oksana were both inconsolable. Aleksander tried everything to comfort them, from taking them on a vacation trip at Koblevo Beach to lavishing gifts and trinkets on them both. Nothing would suffice.

"Oksana," Aleksander told her several weeks later, sitting on the edge of her bed, "I've been noticing that you're excelling in language studies. Since you've had to give up your dream, at least for now, maybe you'd like to focus on becoming a linguist and translator?"

"But Tato, I hate to give up on skating."

"I know you're heartbroken, Oksana. Maybe you can return to skating after you're completely healed. But think about the recovery time ahead of you, my pet. During that time, you can excel in your language studies and have the possibility of a second career without the danger of such profound injuries. Wouldn't that be wonderful?"

His encouragement boosted her mood somewhat. "All right, Tato," she conceded. "I'll think about it."

"Excellent, my pet. See here? I've bought you some language CDs of Ukrainian, Russian, and American English to keep you occupied while you're laid up. And here are library books of short stories in each to help you excel."

"Thank you, Tato," she agreed, to please him. She didn't sound overjoyed at the prospect of giving up on a skating career. She already spoke Russian at home, Ukrainian at school, and was learning English, as were all young Ukrainians. But she could learn a good deal more about the intricacies of grammar and composition of each.

Fortunately, Oksana soon warmed to her new goal, what with the mountains of time she had to practice languages during her six-month recovery. Although her parents were devastated by her injury, Oksana finally began taking it in stride and started to enjoy studying English especially, toward her *new* goal: a visit to America one day! Her teacher told her she was speaking English almost like an American now. The new hope of traveling to America someday was always on her mind.

"Oksana, I'm so proud of you, sweetheart," Olga told her one day. "You seem to be enjoying your language studies. And your teachers tell me how well you're doing."

Oksana was propped up in bed with her dolls all lined up before her. "Yes, Mama. I like pretending I'm a great teacher and translator. Right now, I'm teaching my dolls how to speak English. Maybe someday I can visit America."

"Oh, Oksana. Don't even think about that now. You're only a child." The thought of her beautiful daughter traveling to the U.S. frightened her.

But as Oksana continued her studies through elementary school and into high school, her English teachers continued to praise her remarkable progress with the language. And Oksana seemed to have found a new calling, one for which she received much encouragement and praise.

Despite Ukraine's teetering independence after the fall of the Soviet Union, Russian agents were always on the lookout for promising candidates for the SVR, the successor to the KGB in foreign intelligence. They sought budding linguists in the secondary schools of Ukraine, speakers of Ukrainian as well as Russian and American English.

The SVR was also surveilling separatists living in Ukraine as potential assets, one of whom was Oksana's father, Aleksander, who had been involved in pro-Russian organizations and had participated in some demonstrations against pro-Kyiv demonstrators. He had been among the group of pro-Russian demonstrators who occupied and then set fire to the Trade Unions House when Oksana was just three months old, a mere month after her baptism.

After that frightening experience, Olga had said, "Aleksander, I'm sorry, but I can't let you participate in any more dangerous demonstrations. Fifty people died! It could have been you, love! I don't want you risking your life, especially now that we're parents of such an exceptional child. She needs her Tato, and I need my husband. I could never manage on my own."

Aleksander had reluctantly agreed. He felt a kinship with his pro-Russian colleagues, but not nearly as much as he loved Olga and Oksana. "Yes, I guess you're right, kitten. It's time for me to leave this activism to the younger generations," he said, looking up from his newspaper. "I'm afraid the conflict is getting worse every day. I'll keep saying my prayers for the separatists, but I won't risk my life needlessly again, I promise."

"Thank you, my love," she said, bending down to kiss him tenderly. "I'll try my best to make it up to you."

"Ha," said Aleksander with a wink. "I'll make sure you do."

⅄

Oksana, reared by pro-Russian sympathizers, naturally grew up believing that the Russians had been wronged after the Soviet fall. Of course, the SVR knew of Aleksander and his earlier pro-Russian activities. They knew he had given up demonstrations, so he was no more use to them. Now they had their eyes on his daughter instead, a beautiful young Russian sympathizer, as she grew and thrived in her language classes. Perhaps she could be molded into the perfect Russian Agent.

When Oksana, a tall, stunning, blue-eyed teenager, was in her third and last year in secondary school, her loyalty to Russia, along with her exceptional aptitude in languages, caught Andrei Andropov's eye. Andropov, the Deputy Director of a language school in Moscow, had easy access to Oksana's high school through one of his mistresses, Ana Ivanova, Oksana's English teacher.

Since Russians could still travel easily to Ukraine after the Soviet dissolution, Andropov often flew to Odesa to visit Ana, combining "business and pleasure," as he liked to say.

"My beautiful Ana," he said over wine one night at dinner, "I absolutely adore you, you know. We must see each other more often. Perhaps you can fly to Moscow soon?"

"Ah, Andrei, you know I can't leave my classes. Maybe this summer I can visit, sometime when we're both free. But for now, the classes take all my time."

This was Andrei's cue to change the subject to her classes. And to Oksana, his real reason for this visit to Odesa. "Speaking of your classes, my sweet, I've watched Oksana Kovalska grow into a charming young woman, and I've learned of her remarkable progress in English and Russian."

"Yes, she is undoubtedly my best student," Ana agreed. "She's a hard worker. Very committed."

"I'd like you to arrange an interview for me with her parents. Would you do that, love? I believe she would be the perfect candidate for our language institute."

"A wise choice, Andrei. She'd do well in your language school. I'll speak to her father on your behalf. He's extremely proud of her, you know, so I suppose he'll welcome the chance to brag about her skills."

"Wonderful, darling. Did I ever tell you, you're the best?"

"The best out of all your other women?"

"Don't be silly, my pet." He picked up her hand to kiss it.

After dinner and a few glasses of wine, Andrei became quite amorous. "Perhaps you could put on that album by Yulya I like so much."

"Are you trying to seduce me, you silly goat?"

"That is my profoundest hope," he replied with a sly grin.

Soon he had wooed her into her bedroom, where he slowly disrobed her, stopping to kiss each portion he uncovered while the strains of "The Little Blue Kerchief" completed the magical, sensuous mood. He also disrobed and pulled Ana gently down on the bed beside him, where they embraced, kissing passionately and writhing together in unison. Ah, she was a marvelous lover. Soon, his passion reached such heights that he lost all control and ravaged her body gloriously. Afterward, the couple lay snuggled and panting. Ana sighed, "My Andrei, you are the best lover ever. If only we could be together always."

"Yes, yes," he assured her in his own afterglow.

"Someday we'll be together." Of course, Andrei Andropov had never been accused of being 100 percent honest.

During his first visit to the Kovalskis' modest apartment, in fact, Agent Andropov presented them with a less than accurate picture of Oksana's future possibilities. He didn't lie, he told himself, just made a few tactical omissions.

"Allow me to introduce myself—I'm Andrei Petrovich Andropov, Deputy Director of the Yuri Gagarin Language Institute in Moscow," he said with a slight bow of his head and a wide smile. "I'm a professional colleague of Ana Ivanova, Oksana's English teacher. Every year, Ms. Ivanova alerts me to the most promising language students as potential scholarship recipients of our prestigious language institute. She has confirmed Oksana's natural ability with English and Russian. Because of Oksana's excellence and commitment to hard work, we're pleased to offer her a full scholarship."

Olga gasped. "How wonderful! A full scholarship! But Moscow?"

"Yes, Moscow. Rest assured, she would live in our closely supervised women's dormitory. She'd also be allowed to return to her family for two months in the summer and a month in December."

"How long would she be away?" Aleksander asked.

"The program lasts for two years. After that, exceptional Ukrainian graduates are placed in important posts in your Ukrainian diplomatic corps." He didn't like bordering on the truth, but he knew it was the most likely way to convince the Kovalskis. "What do you think of this generous offer?"

Olga looked to Aleksander and exclaimed, "All the way to Moscow? But she's only seventeen!"

"I assure you, Madame," Andrei interjected, "our young female students are meticulously supervised by certified dormitory house mothers who zealously guard them from unwelcome advances by any would-be suitors or other untoward predators. She will be completely safe."

What Andrei neglected to reveal was that being safe at school did not necessarily mean being safe in the field after graduation.

Olga glanced at Aleksander, a skeptical look on her face.

"Mr. Andropov," said Aleksander, "we're honored by the offer, but we need to consider what Oksana wants." He turned to his daughter, who was sitting expectantly on the edge of the ottoman. "Oksana, my pet, is this something you'd want to do? Before you answer, please realize you'd be far away from your family for a long time."

Oksana, bursting with excitement, clapped her hands together and said, "Oh, Tato, I'm thrilled by the offer. I'd love to go to the language institute and have a future in the diplomatic corps! Please, Mama and Tato! Please, please! I'll make you both proud of me, I promise!"

Glancing over at his sullen wife, Aleksander said, "Mr. Andropov, we're flattered by your offer, but it's a big decision. We need to discuss this further before we can agree. You understand."

"Of course, I do. But I urge you not to hesitate too long," said Director Andropov. "An opportunity like this comes along only once in a lifetime. Soon we'll have to offer the scholarship to another student if Oksana doesn't accept it." One can almost picture Director Andropov twirling a Snidely Whiplash mustache.

"We understand. We'll give our answer to Miss Ivanova to relay to you by the end of the week. We have much to discuss."

"Very well, then. Please realize that your acceptance of this extraordinary offer will guarantee Oksana a bright and secure future," said Andrei as he bid good-bye and left the Kovalski's flat, a smug grin on his face.

What Andrei Andropov had neglected to reveal was that the Yuri Gagarin Language Institute was one of the most notorious schools of the SVR, a training academy for Russia's foreign intelligence service. Language instruction was indeed a part of the preparation for foreign intelligence, but only a small part. Ana Ivanova had warned Andrei, "I would caution you not to reveal the foreign intelligence portion of the training since the Kovalskis are so protective of Oksana. Foreign intelligence might tip them off that Oksana will likely be assigned to a secret foreign mission."

The following week was fraught with hemming and hawing as Aleksander and Olga debated the prospect of their only daughter flying to Moscow and staying for two years before going God knows where after that time. They had not even considered that *God knows where* could be somewhere outside of Ukraine.

"We must realize that our little girl is growing up," Aleksander said. "She'll have to find a career and eventually leave the nest. Just think, a full scholarship! How could we ever pay for her to go to college? This is an exceptional opportunity for her, Olga."

"But to Moscow!"

"You know I pray for Ukraine to be returned to Russia, so she'll be well prepared if that day comes."

"But we'll never be able to see her," Olga moaned.

"It isn't forever. She'll be home at Christmas and during the summer. It would be the same if she went off to college in Ukraine, only for four years instead of two. You can't hold on to her forever, my love. Someday, she must fly like a bird."

They brought Oksana into the conversation to make sure she understood what all this meant. Her father encouraged her to take the plunge, while her mother urged her to think long and hard. But Oksana was so excited about the opportunity that no amount of naysaying from her mother could change her mind.

"This is something I'm convinced I must do," she told them. "Nothing can change my mind. You might as well stop trying, Mama."

This was the first time their cherished daughter had demanded anything, so finally, near the end of the week, they allowed themselves to make the fateful decision. Olga would have to give in. After much sobbing and arguing, Oksana had finally stomped her foot and said, "I'm going, and that's all there is to it. I'm old enough to make up my own mind."

Aleksander was pleased for her, of course, though he'd miss her. Olga spent her hours trying to understand Oksana's new defiance. But the choice was made.

That evening, Olga relented tearfully, and Aleksander called Ana Ivanova to say, "Please, Ms. Ivanova, let Mr. Andropov know that we've decided to accept his generous offer. A full scholarship will help us financially to get Oksana the best education possible, and Oksana is beside herself with excitement."

"Wonderful news. I'm sure none of you will be disappointed with the results."

After they hung up, Ana called her lover and said, "Oksana has accepted. I hope I haven't permitted anything that will harm my best student."

"Don't worry, love. All will turn out perfectly."

The following September, Oksana was on her way to Moscow by train for the beginning of her linguistic-slash-espionage training.

CHAPTER 3

MOSCOW, FALL 2012

Upon her arrival at the language institute, Oksana was assigned to a dormitory housing eighty other young women. The men's dorms were strategically placed far across campus from the women's. But before finding their rooms, all the freshmen were ushered into the auditorium for orientation while their luggage was being transported to their various dorm rooms after some secret and random searches for contraband.

Most of the students were from Russia, but since Oksana's primary language was Russian, she fit in immediately and spoke easily with the young women on either side of her in the cavernous conference room that buzzed with nervous chatter.

"Are you nervous?" one girl beside Oksana asked her in Russian.

"Terrified. I've never been away from home," said Oksana. "But I'm also excited. And you?"

"Da, I'm nervous, too. I've never been away from

Omsk. Where are you from?"

"I'm from Odesa, a very long way from here."

"I'm from right here in Moscow, but I'm scared, too," said the girl on the other side of Oksana.

As the students looked over their programs, Oksana realized classes other than languages appeared on her course schedule. A course in Russian history, an economics class, but also there was a class called Covert Communications. Oksana was beginning to realize this program's sole emphasis was not on foreign languages.

"Covert Communications?" she asked the girls beside her.

They both just shrugged and screwed their faces into a wordless "I don't know," as a speaker approached the podium to introduce the director.

Oksana was curious, but not overly concerned. After all, if she was headed for a career in the diplomatic service, she must be proficient not only in her language specialty but also in the social sciences. But why covert communications? It sounded secretive, like a spy movie.

Director Andrei Andropov walked to the podium. "Ladies and Gentlemen," he said, "Welcome to our wonderful Language Institute. Many of you are here expressly to study languages, but young ladies and gentlemen need other knowledge besides languages. That's why we offer a wide ranging and well-rounded education, as you've probably noticed on your class schedules. Of course, languages will be the major part of your education. That's why we have professors from the very countries whose languages you'll be studying. Many of our older agents—er—seasoned diplomatic representatives, never learned to speak their new language without a telltale Russian accent. We've learned that students would be much better served if they could speak the language with no discernible accent, as a native would speak. That is our goal for you."

Andropov droned on and introduced some of the teachers as students began yawning and fidgeting until, at last, they were excused to find their rooms.

After sitting through the interminable orientation, Oksana was no more certain of what to expect than before. Feeling more *dis*oriented than oriented, she found her stark dorm room and met her roommate, Svetlana Kuznetsova, from St. Petersburg. Svetlana had also been recruited from a secondary school; her outstanding aptitude was in English and Mandarin.

"I'm glad to meet you, Svetlana," Oksana said in Russian. "I'm also studying English, so maybe we can practice speaking English together?"

"Yes, but please call me Lana. I'm sure we'll be fast friends. May I call you Zena?"

"I suppose so," Oksana said, surprised at being given a nickname so suddenly. She'd never had a nickname before, nor felt the need for one. "Can I ask you a few questions?" She sat on the edge of her bed and signaled for Lana to sit beside her. "What are your thoughts about the course of studies they described?"

"Why do you ask? I haven't given it any thought. We haven't even started classes yet."

"I know, but did you notice we'll be taking a class in covert communications? What has that got to do with becoming linguists or translators?"

"Well, Zena, I assume that working for the diplomatic service might require secret communications sometimes. Doesn't that seem logical to you? Not everyone can be a translator, you know." Her response belied some sarcasm, but Oksana soldiered on.

"I don't know, Lana, it just seems like we're being trained for something more than just linguists or translators. I wonder if they've been completely honest with us."

"We can all serve our countries in our own way. I loyally serve Russia in whatever capacity they choose. I think we should withhold judgment until we know more. I wouldn't question it if I were you. There could be consequences."

Consequences? What sort of consequences? It occurred to Oksana that her training might be for a career much more involved and clandestine than simply Ukrainian diplomacy.

A month into the school year, as Oksana was becoming more settled in her classes, Director Andropov announced before an assembly of all the first-year students: "Ladies and gentlemen, I've come to explain our mission in more detail. You can be proud to learn that those of you who achieve our high standards have been chosen to be special agents of the SVR, a very prestigious opportunity." A collective gasp arose from many of the students, though most, including Lana, knew exactly why they were there. "You'll be assigned to various countries, depending on your language studies, for various purposes."

Oksana was disappointed about Director Andropov's deception, but not surprised. It should have been obvious from the start. Hopefully, her parents wouldn't be terribly upset. Hadn't her father encouraged her to improve her

Russian and told her about his belief that Kyiv was the true birthplace of Russia? And that Ukraine should not be cozying up to the West and NATO? Hadn't Ukraine's economy suffered until takeovers by the wealthy Russians? Maybe it would be Andropov's wish for her to become an agent of the SVR because that might be good for Ukraine as well as for Russia. And, of course, Lana encouraged her in these sentiments.

As the school term progressed, Oksana excelled in all her subjects. She had a month-long winter visit to see her parents between semesters, during which she learned that her father supported her career path.

"Oksana, maybe you can pick up where I had to leave off in support of our true homeland, Russia," he said. "There may be some peril, but I'm sure they won't endanger young women as they might young men. All I can do is urge you to take all necessary precautions and remember what it would do to your mother and me if anything happened to you. I think we should keep this mission from your mother, though, at least for now. She worries about you, you know. And remember, if ever you're unhappy, you can always come home. I'll see to that."

Oksana knew how bitter her father had been since the failed privatization of the pipeline company in Odesa, where he was a mid-level manager. Owners at the main office in Luhansk were pleased when wealthy Russians purchased the company before it went bankrupt. Otherwise, Aleksander would have been laid off with no safety net.

"Very well, Tato," she said, hugging him. "If you're satisfied with my career path, then I'll try to become the best SVR agent I can." She wasn't completely convinced, but then, she wanted to please her Tato.

When she returned to school after her break, she was approached by Director Andropov about a brief mission the following summer on the coast of the Sea of Azov.

"Oksana, you're in the top 1 percent of your class now as you near the end of your first year," he told her. "But I'm sure you'll agree that book learning and theory must be augmented with real-life experience in the field. We'll be sending you on a holiday to a beach resort on the Sea of Azov for a week next August."

Oksana perked up. "A holiday? On a beach?"

"Yes. A working holiday, shall we say? You'll be making contact with a Ukrainian-American professor who will be visiting Ukraine, purportedly for academic research. We suspect he may have another agenda, so we've been tracking his movements for some time. You'll get more detailed instructions later, but for now, you must keep this assignment secret, telling no one, not even your classmates, or Svetlana, or your parents. Your discretion is crucial to the success of this mission, as well as to your future advancement."

"Thank you for your vote of confidence in me," Oksana answered breathlessly, excited about a holiday at a beach resort, even if somewhat nervous about the mission. "I assure you I'll do my best. And you can rely on me to keep it confidential."

"I knew we could."

⅄

Toward the end of April, Oksana was summoned back to the director's office to receive more specific instructions regarding her upcoming mission.

"Please close the door," he said when Oksana entered. "We have a slight change in plans. We've decided to send your roommate, Svetlana, with you on your mission. We've concluded it would be improper for a 19-year-old girl to travel alone to a beach resort. I've just briefed Svetlana on her role as your companion, traveling with you on a brief beach holiday between your school terms. She will have no active role in contacting your target but will serve only to lend the mission authenticity."

"Good. I'll be glad to have a companion. Svetlana and I have become good friends."

"That's what I thought. We want your meeting with your target to look like a chance encounter, just two friends enjoying a holiday at the beach. Of course, we'll be tracking your target's phone on GPS. Your assignment is to be flirtatious with your contact. After you loosen him up a bit with your feminine wiles, you are to ask him where he works. He'll tell you he's a professor in the U.S. Then you must tell him how much you've always wanted to study in the U.S., and could you possibly come to his college on a student visa? We'll get you the visa, of course. Once you have his agreement to act as your reference, you'll suggest exchanging email addresses and promise to apply for the requisite student visa for the school year. Do you think you can complete this important mission?"

"Yes, Mr. Andropov, and it'll give me a chance to practice my English." She didn't reveal her excitement about a beach vacation and a possible trip to the U.S., the place she'd long dreamed of visiting.

"Meanwhile, finish out this spring term with flying colors, just as you have been doing, and get ready for your holiday at the beach in August, da?" Andropov smiled as though this would be a wonderful all-expenses-paid vacation for her. "I'll keep you and Svetlana informed about your travel plans as we get closer to the date of your departure." He patted her on the back as he walked her to the door.

Andropov was right. This assignment would be a welcome respite from the drudgery of her studies. She couldn't help giggling all the way back to her dorm.

Following Andrei Andropov's announcement of the acceleration of Oksana's and Svetlana's training, Oksana noticed a marked change in emphasis in their course of studies.

"Lana," remarked Oksana one afternoon after class, "were you surprised to learn that we'll start a class in self-defense techniques next week? Do you suppose we'll need to become proficient in hand-to-hand combat?"

"Well, the scope of our training was bound to expand," answered Svetlana. "After all, we're being dispatched as full-fledged agents of the SVR, not mere translators. We've got to be realistic about our mission. There could be a time we'll need to know self-defense. We need to learn the techniques as if our life depends on it. Because it may, Oksana."

"First, I'm told to be flirtatious, then I'm supposed to take self-defense courses?"

"We have to be prepared in case this young man should suspect something and become aggressive. Or for any other danger. Like having our mission discovered."

"That's what I like about you, Lana. You tell it like it is, and I know you won't lie to me." Oksana had never even dared to think there could be danger.

CHAPTER 4

SUMMER 2013

Mykola had been hoping to return to Ukraine ever since his dissertation research, and finally, eighteen years after leaving Ukraine, he was preparing to continue his current research there. Could he really have been in the U.S. for eighteen years? He had spent the previous summer on a research fellowship at Harvard with the Ukrainian Research Institute, and now, at last, he was making his travel plans to Ukraine. He had been in the process of writing an academic paper about Russia and Ukraine since the end of Soviet rule, which he hoped to extend into a book and to finally earn a promotion from associate to full professor. Last summer at Harvard, he had been shocked to read allegations that the American lobbyist Paul Manafort worked for Yanukovych and the anti-NATO Party of Regions, which had helped install partisan Russian plants acting as Ukrainians. One of the Russian missions was to attack United States Marines who had been sent to try to bring NATO and Ukrainian troops together. The attacks were severe enough to prevent the Marines from making it to either their base or their ships, so the mission was aborted. The Party of Regions had falsely propagandized the attacks as being caused by angry Ukrainians rather than by Russian plants. Mykola could see that he had much research to do in Ukraine besides searching for the lost nuke.

Meanwhile, Sarah had become jealous of his excitement over the trip the last few months and impatient with his constant researching. "Since you clearly don't have time for me," she told him, "I need someone who cares more about me than his next research trip and getting his next paper published. I'm not getting any younger, Myko, and I want to get married and start a family soon."

"I understand, Sarah. I promise I'll spend more time with you."

"It's too late, Myko. You've promised me too many times. Last summer it was Harvard; this summer it's Ukraine. I honestly have no desire to be dragged to a country so full of unrest, even if it does have a beach. It never ends! I'm sorry, Myko, I didn't want to hurt you. But the fact is, while you were constantly researching, I finally met someone who does have time for me."

"What? Sarah, no! Really? I had no idea! I . . . I don't know what to say. We've been so close! Even while I was researching, I thought about you constantly. I planned to propose as soon as I make full professor and can support you as I'd like to."

"I'm sorry, Myko. I really am. I'm afraid I just don't

have the feelings for you I once had."

"Oh, Sarah, don't say that. I don't want to see you go." He took hold of her shoulders to pull her close, but she wriggled away. "You've meant everything to me, Sarah. Are you sure this is right for you?"

"Yes, 100 percent sure. I'm so sorry. Goodbye, Myko." She pecked him on the cheek, and then she was gone.

Mykola was disconsolate when she walked out and for the rest of the school year. He had tried; truly, he had. But she had become more demanding of his time recently. And maybe he'd become less willing to cater to her whims. He had to admit to himself that he had put his research ahead of her. But his research was essential to his livelihood, maybe even to the future of his homeland. If he waited any longer to go to Ukraine, he might be too late. Situations there were rapidly deteriorating. He scolded himself for thinking he'd have room in his life for a girlfriend.

As a consolation, Mykola knew visiting with his best school friend would cheer him up over his loss. He had emailed Vladyslav in March and been invited to stay with him for the summer in Simferopol, Crimea. Of course, Mykola wasn't aware, nor would he have been shocked, that their correspondence was intercepted by the SVR. Hence, the SVR's plans to have Oksana meet him there.

President Yanukovych had been in power in Ukraine since 2010, thanks to grooming by Paul Manafort to look the part of an honest politician and to spout propaganda palatable to Ukrainians. Much to the dismay of a large portion of the population, Yanukovych had failed to establish closer relations with the EU as he had falsely promised during his campaign, instead strengthening ties with Russia.

During 2011, there had been talk of Russia planning to annex Crimea, but Putin needed a pretext for the invasion. He was waiting until he could claim he was defending the Ukrainian separatists, whom he was covertly supporting with unmarked Russian troops in eastern Ukraine.

Unrest among Ukrainians continued to grow against Yanukovych. Disinformation campaigns, such as the staged riot against American Marines by partisan plants, became all the pretext Putin needed to invade Crimea. Putin's secret desire, many believed, was to reconstitute the Soviet Union, as well as to make sure no former Soviet republic was ever accepted into NATO or the European Union.

Mykola worried about his friend Vlad, with so much tension building in the region. Vladyslav, having taken a similar educational path as Mykola, was now a professor of sociology at Simferopol Economic and Humanitarian Institute in Crimea. Besides getting the chance to connect with his best friend, the university library would be the perfect place for Mykola to continue his research. But they both knew that time was limited before Russia would conduct its expected invasion of Crimea.

When Mykola arrived in Simferopol that June, Vlad met him at the airport, all smiles and robust hugs. Mykola had registered for a 90-day visit.

"Myko! It's so great to see you! I hardly recognized you, but that black hair of yours gave you away. How the hell are you, buddy? It's been too long."

"Hah! You've changed a bit yourself since high school. Looks like life is treating you well. How are things in

Ukraine these days?"

"Not good, I'm afraid. There's been so much unrest that I fear for my country. But let's not talk about that now. You must be starving. Let's go grab a bite to eat and catch up, eh, old pal?"

Vlad took him to Avtokafe, not far from the airport. "So, good buddy, tell me what you're doing these days," Mykola said after they'd settled in and ordered.

"I've also been researching, Myko. The constant life of the professor, no?"

"Indeed. I've been researching so much my girlfriend left me!"

"Oh, that's never good. Are you very sad?"

"I was hurt, of course. I guess I'll remain a confirmed bachelor," he said with a chuckle, trying to make light of his broken heart. "Women are too dangerous for me."

"I agree. I also lost my lover last year. She was opposed to my activism. She said she didn't want to be a war widow."

"I hope your activism is not as dangerous as women," Mykola said.

"Well, we'll have to wait and see about that."

"And I hope war is not imminent."

"We'll have to wait and see about that, too."

After a good night's rest, Mykola had recovered from his jet lag, so Vlad took him to the university library. In fact, they spent most days researching at the library. But they always saved time for catching up afterward over an Obolon lager at a nearby pub, where they commiserated about their failures at having a love life, but mostly about the precarious situation in Ukraine and Crimea.

"Do you really think Ukraine is heading for war?" Mykola asked.

"It looks more and more like it. Situations here are developing very much like the Russian war with the Georgia Republic in '08. I predict the first to go will be Crimea, so I'm considering leaving my job here and moving to Kyiv as soon as I can."

"I can see the similarities to Georgia."

"In any case, the similarities were too much for my lovely Kateryna. I miss her, but I can't blame her."

"In my case, I was told my researching didn't leave me enough time for Sarah. She'd already gone off and found someone else before she even told me! Who does that?"

"Ouch! But professors must publish continually if they ever hope to succeed in the university," Vlad said. "I guess some women just can't cope. Neither with research nor with war. I guess they prefer to go to fancy places, get fine presents and lots of attention," he joked. "Life these days can't be like that. I just don't have the time for a woman anymore. Bah!"

"I guess you're right. I have plenty to keep me busy. In fact, I need to do some exploring on Kerch Peninsula. Any chance you'd like to join me? Maybe we could catch some fish, like in the good old days, before we were bothered by women or war."

"Of course, Myko. We can take my tent and two fishing poles so we can bum around for a day or two. Let's go this weekend! I'm very much in need of some R and R."

"We could both use some of that."

⅄

That Saturday, while they were setting up camp on the beach, Vlad asked, "How's your research coming along? Having any breakthroughs?"

"For one thing, I've learned it was a good thing my family left Ukraine when we did. I wish your family had done the same, especially now that tension is building with Russia."

"It's a big concern of mine, too. How do you like living in the U.S?"

"I miss home sometimes, but I've gotten used to it. I guess you can say I've enjoyed the U.S.—until Sarah moved out. Of course, trying to enlighten my students keeps me busy. At least the ones who want to be enlightened."

"If you're fortunate enough to have the ones who want to be enlightened," Vlad said wryly.

"The majors in PoliSci are usually interested. It's just the ones who take it as an elective."

"Yes, I know the ones. We have some of those here, too."

"I guess no one's immune."

"Why did you bring this metal detector with you, Myko?" Vlad asked when Mykola took it out of his backpack and unfolded it.

"I've been wanting to tell you," Mykola said. "I've never told anyone else, so I need you to keep this to yourself, OK?"

"Of course! If you live in Ukraine, you learn to keep secrets, no?"

"Point taken. So, when the bomb cyclone hit in '94, it swept some Soviet nuclear bombs into the sea. One from the ship my father was on was never found. I'm sure you know about it. I've come to look for it."

"I do remember that one was never found. And you hope to find the bomb with this . . . contraption?"

"Possibly, though I'm not terribly optimistic. I'm hoping that maybe the wave action might have carried the bomb here where it could have been buried during the years since the accident. This detector is waterproof up to ten feet deep, so I'll do most of my searching in shallower water in the general area where Tato told me it was lost. If I don't find it, I guess I'll have to learn how to scuba dive," he said, only half-joking.

"I scuba dive!" Vlad said, brightening. "If you don't find it, maybe I can help you."

"I'll cover as much of the peninsula as I can this summer. If I don't find it, maybe I'll take a scuba course at home and come back next summer. That is, unless Russia gets more aggressive by then. Maybe you'd be my scuba buddy?"

"Of course, I'll be your scuba buddy, Myko!" Vlad said, smiling widely and patting Mykola on the back.

"Deal!" Mykola said. Bending down, he pulled a small cellphone-shaped item out of his backpack.

"Another contraption?" Vlad asked. "How many contraptions do you have in there?"

"This, my friend, is a Geiger counter. If we're lucky enough to find the nuclear bomb after all these years, we could find that it's damaged or rusted. In that case, there's a risk of radioactive seepage. If it registers on this meter, we'll have to abort the mission. Exit stage left STAT."

"You're right! That hadn't even occurred to me. Let the Russians find it instead."

⅄

After their camp was organized, they ambled along the north side of Kerch Peninsula, Mykola in water above his knees.

"Where's your research leading you?" Vlad asked, walking on the beach beside him.

"I'm looking at the rise of fascism and the turn to the far right in eastern Slavic countries as well as much farther abroad," Mykola said. "The trend is startling. I'm trying to see where it might lead, particularly in Ukraine. In my dissertation research, I studied Putin's terrifying philosophy as he's taken it from the fascist philosopher, Ivan Ilyin. It's disturbing and gives me a lot of insight into what Putin's doing now. Do you know of Ilyin?"

"Of course, I know Ilyin's philosophy all too well: the idea that once social mobility ends, democracy is supplanted by oligarchy. The ultimate goal of the oligarchs is to end social mobility and the middle class."

"I fear for Ukraine as I fear for the world," Mykola said. "Ilyin's philosophy points to the danger in all hyper-partisan societies. It gets more frightening daily as we see militias building around the world, even in the U.S."

"I agree," said Vlad. "Putin cites Ilyin to explain why Russia must invade Ukraine and erode the West. Here we're influenced strongly by oligarchy and the far right, while oligarchs give lip service to our nonexistent democracy."

"From what I've read, Yanukovych is just a puppet of Putin." Myola stooped and pulled up a rusted can. "Ach. So far, all I'm coming across out here is garbage." He tossed the can onto shore, and Vlad put it in the trash bag he was carrying for that purpose.

They continued searching and commiserating for a mile or two until Mykola said, “Let’s turn back for now. I can continue my search on the way back to camp. I have a long way to go, but I have all summer. Let’s go have a brew and some grub, maybe catch a fish. We need to make this time together a vacation, too.”

“What if you don’t find the bomb? Your heart will be broken?”

“I’ll be disappointed. But I’ve prepared myself for that. It’s like looking for a needle in a haystack.”

“Needle where?”

“Oh, it’s a U.S. expression. Finding a needle in a haystack.”

“Yes, it would be hard to find a needle there.”

“We’ve found lots of change, an earring or two, beer cans, but nothing useful. Here, you can have the change.”

When they got back to camp, they each popped open an Obolon and fished until they had caught a small stringer of perch and whitefish. As the sun was sinking lower, Vlad got out his camping skillet, oil, and a plastic bag with flour to coat the fish. He had come prepared with a one-burner camp stove, utensils, chips, and a small cooler of bottled water and Obolon lager to wash down the fish they fried.

They prepared a meal fit for a king, or at least a couple of sand princes. When they sat on a log to eat, Vlad said, “Listen Myko, I have some scuba gear you can use since you’ll be wading. I have a mask, snorkel, and headlamp. I also have an underwater camera, in case you find the bomb.”

“Fantastic. Bring that stuff next time, OK? Just in case.”

“Sure thing.”

They built a campfire and sat on the log beside it to down another brew, watch the sun set, and discuss Ukraine’s plight.

CHAPTER 5

Mykola was unaware that the SVR was surveilling him via GPS and had been since 2002 when he was writing his dissertation on Russian aggression in Ukraine. They were keeping a watchful eye on him now, especially since he was nosing around Crimea. Mykola's fellowship at Harvard last summer had alerted the SVR that he was continuing to research Russia's intentions in Ukraine and the rightward drift toward fascism in much of eastern Europe. Hence, the SVR's decision to place their newly minted foreign intelligence officer, having blossomed into a beautiful young woman and language expert extraordinaire, in Crimea, where Mykola is doing his research. She is to use her seductive charms to see where Mykola's research is leading. Russia can never be too careful.

Quite apart from Mykola's writings, the SVR knows that Mykola's father, Bronislav, served in the Ukrainian navy with the Black Sea Fleet, the fleet that lost the suitcase bomb. Although the nuclear device was no longer operational, it could still function as a dirty bomb, scattering lethal radiation over a wide area, and so potentially useful to both the Ukrainians and the Russians as a deterrent or in the event of a future war—which could happen sooner rather than later.

Mykola was known to be frequenting the very area on Kerch Peninsula where a few of the tactical nuclear weapons had been recovered years ago. Did Bronislav tell Mykola the location of the "Broken Arrow," as the loss or theft of a bomb has come to be called? Is Mykola searching for the one remaining lost bomb, and is he working on behalf of Ukraine? Or the CIA? They needed to find out.

CHAPTER 6

Near the end of summer, after several exasperating weekends with the metal detector, Mykola finally had to acknowledge that his search had been a chimera. As the pair packed their backpacks to head to the university library, Vlad said, "You know, Myko, we need a break from study, and also from your contraption. You're working too hard. Look outside! The sun's shining; it's a beautiful day. Instead of staying cooped up in a stuffy library, let's go and relax in the sun, yes? I can also take my tent if you like. But no working allowed. Deal?"

"Deal! You're right, Vlad. I'm too exasperated to work right now."

They unloaded the books and papers from their backpacks and replaced them with swimsuits and beach towels. Vlad also packed his camping equipment, picnic food, and Obolon and drove them to his favorite secluded beach on Kerch Peninsula, just west of Tatarka Beach. Of course, the SVR knew exactly where they were.

After they set up camp, Vlad ushered Mykola to his

favorite spot at the far western end of the beach where it was less crowded. They unrolled their towels, turned on Vlad's portable radio, and spread out to catch some rays. Stretching out on the warm sunny beach was a welcome respite when they needed it most, though it was hard for Mykola to clear his mind of all he had hoped to do. He expected pro-Russian separatists to escalate their aggression alongside the unmarked Russian troops amassing at the border and in eastern Ukraine. It would be an unprecedented disaster if they found and detonated the dirty bomb in one of the large cities. It could even rival the Chernobyl disaster in northern Ukraine in '86.

"Is your family worried about all the war drums beating?" he asked Vlad

"Of course, they're worried. But they've resigned themselves to staying. I'd probably be accepted in the U.S. with my degree, but I can't bring myself to leave my comrades or my family behind."

"I understand, but I wish you could all come. I worry about your safety, Vlad."

After an hour of swapping stories and sipping Obolon, they noticed two beautiful young women approaching them, like a vision, in lacy beach cover-ups over skimpy swimsuits.

"Excuse me for being so bold, but you're getting burned," said one of the women when they reached the two men.

"Ah, right you are," said Mykola, looking down at his chest. He stood up to pull on his T-shirt and shorts over his swimsuit. "Now, that's better, yes?"

Vlad followed suit, hopping on one leg to pull his shorts onto the other leg.

"Yes, much better. I would hate to see such handsome young men get all sore from a sunburn. It would be a shame to peel. Don't you agree, Lana?" Oksana asked, smiling at her companion.

Svetlana agreed and took her cue to introduce themselves. "I'm Svetlana," she said, moving closer to Vlad. "And this is my roommate, Oksana. May we ask your names?"

"It's nice to meet you both," said Mykola, grinning widely at the welcome intrusion. "I'm Mykola and this is my good pal, Vlad."

"So, Mykola," Oksana said, sidling closer to him. "I sense by your accent that you're not from Ukraine?"

"Oh, yes, I *am* from Ukraine. Originally. I moved to the U.S. when I was 17, so I'm afraid my Ukrainian has suffered in the bargain."

At this, Svetlana pouted and said to Vlad, "I see those two want to visit. Would you like to take a walk with me, Vlad? I still need to get some more exercise."

Not one to turn down such an offer, Vlad slipped on his sandals and fibbed, "I was just thinking of taking a walk myself."

After those two wandered off, Oksana continued fulfilling her assignment, thinking, *at least he is handsome. This assignment might be fun.*

"The U.S.?" she said. "That must be an exciting place to live. And what do you do in the U.S.?"

"I'm a professor of political science. I study current political issues in Ukraine and other countries. I try to point out parallels between various countries wherever I see them. Lately, Ukraine is much in the news."

"So, you discuss with your students in the U.S. about political issues in Ukraine?"

"And other places, as well. We're all interconnected in a way. I'll admit to having a soft spot in my heart for Ukraine, and I'm concerned about the unrest they're having now."

"You're so lucky," Oksana said wistfully. "I've always wanted to visit the U.S. In fact, I wish I could go there for my studies, perhaps in a Studies Abroad program. I wonder if it would be very difficult to get into one of those programs?"

"I'm sure you could easily get in if you really wanted to. Maybe you should apply for a student visa. What's your area of interest?"

"I've studied English and Russian for several years already. Languages are my main interest, but I think I'll need to take courses in political science to learn more about the politics of various countries. Where do you teach?"

Oksana began ambling toward a small berm, so Mykola followed, and they sat side by side. "I teach at a mid-sized university in Ohio," he said.

"I'd prefer not to go to a huge university. I'd be too intimidated. Do you think I could get into your university?"

"It's a very selective school, but with your language skills and interests, I don't think you'd have any trouble getting accepted. I assume you do have good grades?"

"Oh yes. I'm at the top of my class," she said proudly.

"You could use my name as a reference if you're

sincere about making such a big move. I always tell my students it's important for them to study abroad for at least a semester, if possible, to broaden their minds. I think it would be good for you to see the wider world."

"I'd like very much to broaden my mind. Would it be all right if I took your class? I wouldn't be so intimidated if I had a friend from Ukraine to teach me," she said, smiling coyly at him.

"I'd be honored to have you in my class," he said. "Would you plan to come this fall?"

"Oh, no. I have one more year of my language training," she said. "It would be the fall of 2015."

"Well, then, I'll be looking forward to seeing you if you decide to come."

"Oh, thank you! I'm excited now that I might be going to America!" Oksana said, clapping her hands together and beaming up at him.

"Oh look, Vlad and Svetlana are walking back this way," Mykola said. "I guess since we're getting burned, we should probably think about packing up."

"Where are you staying?" she asked, ignoring his hint to leave. "With Vlad?"

"Yes, we're best friends from when I lived here. He teaches in Simferopol now."

"But you haven't even told me your last name?"

"My last name is Kravchenkos."

"So, Professor Mykola Kravchenkos. A beautiful Ukrainian name for a beautiful Ukrainian man," she said seductively. "Please, let's exchange emails so I can ask you for some help with enrolling. What was the name of the college, by the way?"

"Youngstown State University, in Ohio." Mykola was

startled by her coquettish behavior but certainly not averse to it.

They exchanged emails using their phones. "I know you don't know me, but would you consider writing me a reference letter? I assure you, I'm in the top 1 percent of my class. I'd be an excellent student at your college."

No lack of self-confidence, he thought. "I'd be happy to. Perhaps you could send me a transcript? Then I'd have something concrete to include in the letter."

"Yes. I'll do that as soon as I get back to Odesa."

As Vlad and Svetlana approached the pair, Vlad asked with a knowing smirk, "Well, becoming friends, are we?"

"Yes, Oksana is thinking of coming to study at Youngstown State U!" Mykola said, giving his friend a nod to illustrate his approval of the idea.

"Ah! That sounds like a good plan. I think all students who are able should study abroad. And now wouldn't be a bad time to get out of Ukraine for a while, until we see if things cool down here," Vlad said, smiling at Oksana. He turned to Mykola. "Do you know what Svetlana's been saying? She says she's getting hungry. And I'm hungry, too. We found a little beachfront restaurant about a half kilometer down the beach. Why don't the four of us go eat something and maybe share a bottle of wine?"

"Ooh!" piped up Oksana, looking wide-eyed at Mykola. "What do you think, Professor Kavchenkos? Are you hungry as well?"

Choosing not to mention the picnic they'd brought, Mykola said, "Well, I'm not going to be a stick in the mud.

Let's go."

"What is this stick in the mud?" Oksana asked, wrinkling her nose.

"Ah, a serious student of English should know the idioms. A stick in the mud is a party pooper."

"Party pooper?"

"I'll explain on the way."

They walked the half-mile to the Tatapka restaurant and found a table on the terrace overlooking the Sea of Azov.

"Let's eat family style," Oksana suggested. In agreement, they all decided on cold borscht and savory pampushky, donuts sprinkled with garlic. They also ordered varenyky, called pierogis in the U.S., for a second course. And the obligatory wine, of course! They ordered a bottle of Artemovsk, the sparkling wine known by Ukrainians as "Soviet champagne."

After Vlad dished out small bowls of the borscht, they each added a dollop of sour cream. Looking directly at Mykola, Oksana commented, "You know, there's an old saying that no Ukrainian woman will find a husband if she can't make delicious borscht."

Mykola said, "Yes, I know the saying. My mother makes the best borscht I've ever tasted. None have ever compared, in my view. My father always jokes that's why he married her."

"Maybe one day I'll make borscht for you, Professor Kravchenkos," said Oksana.

Mykola didn't take the bait and instead replied, "Well, perhaps one day you can come to my parents' house, and the two of you can have a cook-off. It would delight my father."

Svetlana interjected, "I've heard of Oksana's famous borscht. But Ukrainian borscht can't compete with Russian borscht, I'm sorry!"

Groans and eye rolls all around the table. "We all know of Russian borscht," said Oksana, smiling at her roommate. "Perhaps you and I should have a competition."

A few awkward chuckles escaped as the waiter placed a bowl of sauerkraut and bacon varenyky on the table.

"So much talk of borscht," said Vlad, digging into the bowl. "I prefer varenyky."

Changing the subject from borscht and varenyky, Mykola turned to Oksana and asked, "Tell me, Oksana, what sort of studies have you had at your school? Besides languages, that is."

"Mostly languages, of course, but I've also had Russian history and economics. I've learned a great deal about unrest here in my country. The company where my father works was privatized in 1992."

"After the fall of the Soviet Union."

"Yes. His company was going broke until Russian businessmen bought it and saved it."

"Russian oligarchs?"

"Well, I don't know if they're oligarchs," said Oksana. "My father considers them saviors."

"It was such a period of unrest. I believe the oligarchs got much wealthier," said Mykola. "Have you written any papers in your history or economics class about the unrest? It would be helpful for me to see a sample of your writing if I'm to write you a reference."

"I wrote a paper in history that might serve your

purpose, called 'How Democracies Become Displaced.' Perhaps that would suffice?" She didn't mention that it was more a how-to than a warning.

"Ah, yes. That sounds most interesting and very much in line with my course," said Mykola.

As they were enjoying the last of their wine, Vlad said, "Myko, the sun is getting lower. Maybe we should think about heading back to camp."

Mykola reluctantly agreed. He was quite enjoying Oksana's company. The two men split the bill, said their good-byes to the lovely young women, and parted. It had occurred to Mykola during lunch that Oksana could be a Russian sympathizer. She didn't seem put off by the Russian oligarchs that so inflamed him and Vlad. *Oh well,* he thought, *maybe she would add some spice to his class. At least he might enlighten her.*

CHAPTER 7

The summer was near an end. Mykola and Vlad took one last two-day excursion to Kerch Peninsula. So far this summer, they had found a large bag of kopiyok of different denominations, but when they counted them, the total was only about 15 hryvnias, or just over 26 U.S. dollars, plus bottle openers, eating utensils, and battlefield relics. But no bombs.

They had increased their coverage to four or five kilometers a day, but there were still endless hectares to cover. Vlad took turns with the metal detector when Mykola got tired. Both men were getting worn down by all the beachcombing. They were sunburned, and their feet ached from trudging miles a day in the sand and water.

On the second day of this last excursion, about a meter from shore, the beeping began. *More beer cans,* Mykola thought. He dug a little way down, and the beeping continued. A little deeper, the beeping became louder and more insistent. He got out of the water and handed Vlad the metal detector. He dug the Geiger counter out of his backpack. "Better safe than sorry," he said, placing the device in its clear waterproof case.

"Absolutely," Vlad agreed.

Vlad used the metal detector while Mykola dug deeper and deeper. The beeping grew more persistent. When he got down to about one meter, his shovel clanked against something hard. When he placed the Geiger counter on top of the mud covering the bomb, it began to click, frightening them both. As they watched, the meter ticked up to category 2. They waited, but it never rose above category 2, a range that was above normal but not indicating health danger.

Wearing the mask, snorkel, and submersible headlamp that Vlad lent him, Mykola ducked below the surface. He dug furiously—until there it was! The missing nuke, complete with the muddy, barely discernible Russian insignia of hammer and sickle inside a star! The canvas bag it was transported in had rotted into shreds, but there was no sign the bomb had rusted through or leaked. Mykola placed the Geiger counter directly on the bomb and watched as the level rose slightly but never went above category 2, where the risk of cancer would have increased. Mykola stood up, took off his mask, and shouted for joy as Vlad joined in, the two of them splashing, whooping, and hollering.

Mykola was so overwhelmed that he splashed to shore and plopped down to catch his breath and wipe away a tear of joy. *Now, what do we do?* he thought. It took a few minutes before his brain kicked in again.

"OK, Vlad, I need to borrow your underwater camera for proof. Then I need to cover this up and go to the U.S. Embassy in Kyiv," he finally said. "First, I need to find the coordinates on Google Maps. Or better yet, could you find the coordinates? My phone could be tapped. I'll just jot them on a piece of paper. Then you can delete them in case you're hacked. Safer that way."

"Do you really think they could be surveilling you?"

"Nothing would surprise me."

"This is exciting, Myko! Like espionage. But why go to the U.S. Embassy?"

"I only want American intelligence to get this so they can eliminate the possibility of separatists getting their hands on it."

Vlad found the exact coordinates, and Mykola jotted them down in the pocket notebook in the backpack Vlad was carrying.

"I'll give you a hand covering it up," Vlad said after Mykola snapped a picture. Vlad took the foldable shovel out of the backpack, and standing above waist-deep, he and Mykola shoveled furiously, breathlessly, until the hole was filled and patted down.

The pair returned to camp, packed up all their gear, and headed to Vlad's apartment, where Mykola called the U.S. Embassy in Kyiv to make an appointment for the next day. Then he called the airlines and booked an early flight from Simferopol to Kyiv early that morning.

"Vlad, you've done so much for me this summer. I hate to even ask, but would you mind doing me one more favor before I get out of your hair? Would you drive me to the airport tomorrow morning?"

"Out of my hair?"

"Another American expression. Means I'll stop bothering you."

"You're no bother. You're my best friend, for God's

sake. Of course, I'll drive you. I hope you'll come back before another 18 years, though!" Vlad said.

"Maybe you could visit me in the U.S. next time? Have you ever been?"

"No, I haven't. I'll surprise you and come one day."

"Ha. I hope you do. But I won't hold my breath."

"Anyway, Myko, since this is our last night for who knows how long, let's go out and celebrate your success with a nice dinner and a bottle of wine," Vlad said.

"I concur, but only if you let me treat."

Over dinner, Mykola said, "Vlad, please think seriously about emigrating if situations get any worse. I'll sponsor you. You can come stay with me as long as you need to, and I'm sure you could get a job at my school or another one nearby. Keep your passport up to date and get a visa. I'm serious, Vlad. I worry about you here all the time!"

"I'll think about it. We'll see," Vlad said.

Mykola knew his request was futile.

Before dawn the next morning, Vlad drove Mykola to the airport for his short hop to Kyiv. After their good-byes and promises to visit one another, Mykola boarded, a little sad to be leaving his old friend. But he had found what he had come for and fulfilled his childhood dream. Now he hoped this information would be helpful to the Ukrainians, whether they ever realized it or not. Perhaps better they did not.

His flight landed at 8:00 AM, too early to go to his hotel or the embassy. He grabbed his rolling suitcase and backpack from the carousel, bought a paper, and found an airport coffee shop. He took a seat near the front, never noticing the man reading a paper in the far corner. But the man noticed him. In fact, one SVR agent or another had been keeping a closer eye on him since they learned of his plans to visit his friend.

Mykola had also not noticed the same man on his flight to Kyiv from Simferopol this morning. He was too lost in self-pity over returning to an empty apartment now that Sarah was gone. Maybe it was for the best. Maybe if he'd truly loved her, he'd have found more time to spend with her. He could see why his motives had seemed selfish to her. He'd refused to consider her feelings while he continued his constant research. Now he was paying for his mistakes.

Mykola also thought of Oksana. She was beautiful, and he knew she was attracted to him. He scolded himself for also feeling an attraction to her. Anyway, he rather doubted that she'd really come to Youngstown. Just a passing flirtation, he thought. Probably just a rebound attraction after losing Sarah. Nevertheless, he couldn't get her out of his mind. But no, no, no, he would never contact her. Not unless he heard from her first, this young and lovely Ukrainian woman. He noticed she demonstrated some sympathy toward Russia, but it never occurred to him that Oksana could work for the SVR, though he knew enough never to tell her or anyone but Vlad about the bomb.

At 8:45, he found a taxi and told the driver, "U.S. Embassy, please."

When he arrived, he showed his passport and driver's license to the receptionist and said, "I have an appointment at 9:00 to talk to an American diplomat about what I've found. It is quite urgent."

"Certainly, Mr. Kravchenkos," the young lady behind the information desk said, looking up from the pictures on his passport and license and handing them back to him. "Please have a seat for a moment."

Soon, a tall gentleman approached, and Mykola stood to shake his hand. "Good morning, Mr. Kravchenkos. I'm Agent James Matthews. Please come with me." Mykola followed him into a plush office.

"Now, what would you like to tell me?" he asked after the two were seated.

"I'm a Ukrainian-American from Youngstown, Ohio, a professor at Youngstown State..." And he proceeded to tell Officer Matthews the whole story. How he had moved to the U.S. at 17, how his father had told him the story of the lost nuke, how he had aspired to find it and now had indeed found it buried on the north shore of the Kerch Peninsula.

"Fascinating story. But how would we be able to find this bomb?" asked the officer.

"I've reburied it three feet under the surface. I wrote down the coordinates." He handed Officer Matthews a sheet with the coordinates. "In addition, I've taken a picture with an underwater camera, so that you'll know this is the missing suitcase bomb. You can keep this copy. I printed it before I deleted it. See here? You can barely make out the Russian hammer and sickle inside a star."

"Ah, yes, I see. And why are you showing me this?"

"To make sure you know this isn't a hoax. My purpose

in finding it was to prevent the separatists from finding it and using it on our people. The fuses were removed from all the bombs before transport, so it's not operational anymore, but it could still be used as a dirty bomb and potentially kill a lot of innocent people."

"I agree. You've come to the right place. If you'll please jot down your school address for me, I'll alert my contacts in the U.S. right away. We wouldn't want to call you on your personal phone. Rather, someone will be in touch with you at your school shortly. Now then, I'll ask you not to mention this to anyone. Have you told anyone yet?"

"Only my high school friend, Vladyslav Domitrovich. He's a professor in Simferopol. He was kind enough to let me stay with him while I was in Crimea, and he's been driving me around and helping me search. I know he won't tell anyone."

"Perhaps I'd better have you jot his school address here as well, on the outside chance we need to contact him. OK, Mr. Kravchenkos. Thank you for this information. Someone will be in touch soon. Please tell no one else."

"Absolutely. I'll tell no one."

Mr. Matthews stood and said, "In that case, I'll thank you for coming in. I'll pass this along to American intelligence. Your information could prove to be quite valuable indeed."

They shook hands, and Mykola left, feeling a great sense of pride and relief over what he'd accomplished over the summer. It wasn't a wasted trip, after all. What Agent Matthews had not told him was that he was an undercover CIA agent working at the embassy. Immediately after Mykola left the office, Matthews dialed CIA headquarters at Langley in Virginia on his SatPhone and filled in the duty officer.

⅄

Mykola found his hotel, the Aleksandria, on Google Maps, only 12 minutes' walking distance, so he put on his backpack and rolled his suitcase behind him. He ate lunch in the hotel dining room while he waited until he could check in and jotted some notes in his pocket spiral. He never noticed the man who came in five minutes later and sat several tables away, the same man who had sat in the corner at the airport coffee shop.

CHAPTER 8

Now that the SVR had followed Mykola to the U.S. Embassy, they were certain he had indeed found the missing nuke. Why else would he go to the embassy? The SVR hoped to get to it first and transport it to Russia, its rightful place, before Mykola could succeed in handing it over to the Ukrainian government, or worse, to the Americans. They feared it might be used as a tactical or battlefield weapon against Russian troops and separatists in the coming months.

Mykola knew he was a step ahead of the Russians now that he had the coordinates of the bomb's location. What he didn't know, for certain anyway, were Russia's upcoming plans for Crimea. The Russians, preoccupied with plans and propaganda for that upcoming invasion, had decided to use their carefully chosen undercover agent to pry those bomb coordinates out of Mykola's hands by "trickery and deceit," as Maxwell Smart would say. Someone like the lovely Oksana, linguist and spy extraordinaire.

Meanwhile, the CIA had the exact location of the lost

nuke. They hoped to dig it out of the muck and move it out of reach of the Russians without a large-scale military operation that could trigger a shooting war between the U.S. and Russia. They decided to use the United States Navy Seal Team Bravo. That elite group had already proven its ability to sweep in and out of hotspots undetected. The key was to complete the mission before the Russians discovered the coordinates. Seal Team Bravo could be launched from a Navy ship on routine patrol in the Black Sea, pre-planned by a joint CIA/Pentagon task force.

Besides handing Agent Matthews a copy of the coordinates, Mykola had also jotted them down in his notebook. He planned to lock them in the safe in his office at the university as soon as he got home. By 1 PM the next day, he was in the air on his way to Kennedy airport with the coordinates tucked into the zipper pouch he hung around his neck under his shirt.

CHAPTER 9

Mykola jogged to his office the next morning and placed the bomb coordinates in his safe. He opened his briefcase with the bulging folder of research notes and began the slow process of organizing and incorporating all his new information into his computer.

Although he was up to speed for the first day of fall semester, "Diplomacy in the 21st Century," his mind was laser-focused on how the CIA was proceeding with the bomb. He hoped they'd get in touch soon to tell him the bomb was secured. Despite being preoccupied, he introduced himself to his new students and assigned two readings with emphasis on cybercrime as enabled by intelligence agents in embassies and consulates. Then he let them go on their way.

At their second meeting, he had everyone, including himself, place their desks in a circle. "Cybercrime," he began. "It could mean disrupting or simply threatening to disrupt computers or networks. Terrorist groups can place viruses on entire computer systems or even shut them down completely. Foreign governments can easily surveille other governments, so naturally, the U.S., the largest superpower, is a major target. Russia has already conducted cyber-attacks in Ukraine and in the U.S. Do you believe diplomacy can take place if bad actors are conducting such covert acts? Please state your name until I get to know all of you."

"My name's Liam," said the first to take a stab at it. "In our reading assignment, I saw reports of increased Russian aggression and skirmishes in Ukraine as well as some cyber-attacks on Ukraine's infrastructure. I don't see how diplomacy could work there."

"Russia and Ukraine have been at odds over Crimea since the Soviet break-up," Mykola said. "Russia has also placed unmarked troops in eastern Ukraine. Should the U.S. get involved in the event of war between Russia and Ukraine? Should we try diplomacy first?"

"My name's Connie, and I believe we should at least try diplomacy with Russia. If that doesn't work, couldn't we try sanctions?"

"Of course. We've used sanctions in similar situations. Sometimes, sanctions end up just punishing the population instead of the autocrats," Mykola said, "but sometimes it's our only recourse. One thing we can't do is compromise on our principles. And we have to consider our NATO alliance. Ukraine is not a member, but if NATO should get involved, it could lead to a much wider war."

A lively discussion continued for the full hour, at the end of which Mykola said, "OK folks, your reading assignment for next time is on your syllabus. These are huge problems with no easy solutions. Let's consider several options next time."

⅄

Several weeks into the semester, Mykola received a call at 11 PM from campus security. “Dr. Kravchenkos, this is Lieutenant Mike Schmidt of the Campus Police. At 9:30 this evening, our patrol officer reported that the ventilation grill on your office door had been unscrewed and removed, and someone crawled through the opening. The officer entered your office to check for possible damage or signs of theft. Fortunately, your desk drawer and safe were locked and nothing seemed to be out of place. The officer replaced the grill, so hopefully, whoever it was won’t return and have another go at it.”

“Damn. Well, thanks for letting me know. I’ll check everything in the morning.”

“Sure thing. Also, when the officer went outside to look around, he observed a man in work coveralls walking toward the parking lot at a pretty good clip, carrying what looked like a small tool bag. Our officer ordered the man to stop and questioned him. The man said he was a maintenance contractor working in Haverford Hall, next door to Molson, and was hurrying home after working late on a plumbing issue. He had credentials, so the officer had no grounds to detain him.”

“I hope your guys will keep an eye on it. I have some important stuff in there. Thanks again.”

“OK. Good night, Doc. Oh, by the way, the other thing our officer noticed about him was an accent. Possibly Slavic.”

After the call, Mykola couldn’t get back to sleep. He rolled around for what seemed like hours, his mind refusing to shut down. What if someone was successful next time? He'd have to memorize the coordinate numbers and destroy the paper they were written on.

The next morning, Mykola didn't notice that anything had been disturbed. He confirmed the coordinates were still in his safe. The would-be thief must have been interrupted by someone or something before he could finish the job. Or maybe he simply couldn't open the safe.

Mykola placed the coordinates in the breast pocket of his blazer and left for class. Now he knew the SVR was intent on finding the location of the nuke at any cost. But how could they know he'd found the bomb? Could he and Vlad have been followed?

That evening, after pouring himself a glass of Lambrusco, he took out the coordinates and began contemplating a simple mnemonic. He converted the latitude portion, 45.404843 North, to corresponding letters of the alphabet, DE.DADHDC, which he then committed to memory in a sentence using those letters to begin each word: In the North, Don't Ever Drink A Dreadful Hot Diet Coke—and the longitude component 35.746325 East, CE.GDFCBE, became: In the East, Could Everyone Give Donations For Colorful Balloons Everywhere—silly but easy enough to remember. He would shred the paper and put false coordinates in the safe, a thumb of the nose to any prying Russians who might be better safecrackers, and maybe give the CIA time to find the bomb.

⅄

The CIA was sometimes reluctant to share information with other agencies. Their original intent was to task a Navy Seal Team with retrieving the nuke, but the hand-over was repeatedly bumped by "bigger fish to fry." When the Navy finally got the call, the requested Seal Team was unable to respond.

Although the elite Navy Seal Teams' achievements were celebrated, sometimes strict codes of ethics and morals were compromised. One of the requested Seal Team Bravo members was being investigated for alleged violations of the international rules of war; hence, the team was unable to respond immediately when called. The bomb would just have to wait.

CHAPTER 10

MOSCOW

Russian intelligence services kept their agents in the dark as long as possible before deployment, lest the enemy detect their plans before agents could complete their missions. When Director Andropov decided it was time, he called Oksana into his office.

"Oksana, now is the time to tell you more about your mission and our expectations of you in the U.S. Your main objective is to obtain something from Professor Kravchenkos that is of great value to Russia's glorious quest to be reunited with Ukraine. What I'm about to tell you is critical for Russia's national security, as well as for Ukraine. I must emphasize that you are to reveal this information to no one. Do you understand? Not even Svetlana. Any slips on your part may be detrimental to our goals. And to you personally."

Though Oksana didn't like the sound of that last sentence, she responded, "Yes, sir, I understand." What else could she say?

"The American professor is not just an innocent academic who traveled to Ukraine for research. We have reason to believe he possesses the precise coordinates of a missing Russian nuclear weapon near where you met him last summer. Hundreds of such bombs were deployed all over the Soviet Republics and were ordered to be returned to Russia as part of its denuclearization program. We believe the professor found this 'suitcase bomb,' so named because it was small enough to be transported in a case. He brought a metal detector to Crimea that he was purportedly using to find relics of past wars, while in reality, he was searching, we believe successfully, for the lost bomb. He did not transport the bomb, so we believe it is hidden somewhere in the vicinity of his search.

"Upon Professor Kravchenkos's return to Kyiv," the director continued, "he was observed entering the American Embassy, presumably to report his findings to the CIA agent assigned there. We were unsuccessful in finding the coordinates on Kravchenkos's phone, so we assume he wrote them down and hid them in his university office. Your job is to find and relay these coordinates to your SVR contact at the Russian Consulate in Cleveland, Ohio."

"You mean break into his office?" she exclaimed, startled at the thought.

"Oh, no. How you accomplish this will be up to you, but you might consider breaking down his defenses, not his door, with your obvious feminine charms." He paused to eye her up and down. "Professor Kravchenkos is no doubt emotionally vulnerable following the recent breakup of a longstanding romantic relationship. He should be amenable to your advances. Once we get the coordinates, your presence in the U.S. won't be necessary, and your handler in the Russian Consulate in Cleveland, Demyan Ivanov, will get you on the next flight to Moscow. Here's a burner phone pre-programmed to dial only your SVR contact in Cleveland. The password is *caviar*. Do you have any questions?"

Oksana was surprised at the amount of information she was expected to internalize and assumed it was an indication of how highly the SVR officials regarded her. She resolved to justify their confidence in her.

"I understand how sensitive this information is, sir, and I'll guard it with my life. I believe I can persuade this professor to reveal the coordinates, one way or another."

"Yes, dear, I am certain you can. First, you must send him the transcripts we've prepared for you, leaving out your classes in covert communication and self-defense, of course. Also, send your essay, which we've revised so as not to reveal your true loyalties to Russia. You'll find them as attachments in your email. Save them and attach them to a new email to the professor. Do you understand?"

"Of course."

As the clock ran out on Oksana's SVR training in Moscow and the end of the semester neared for Mykola's students in Ohio, serious unrest and protests had reached a boil at Independence Square in Kyiv: the Euromaidan Revolution of Dignity. By November 2013, thousands of Ukrainians protested the continuing corruption of Yanukovych, their pro-Russian president, who had been strategically placed by Putin. Yanukovych had failed to sign an association agreement with the European Union as promised, opting instead to fulfill his actual agreement with Russia. Thousands of protesters were calling for Yanukovych to step down. Mykola's thoughts turned to his friend Vlad, who would surely join the protests.

CHAPTER 11

Mykola was getting impatient. When would the CIA take action to retrieve the nuke? Would they beat the Russians? Meanwhile, Andrei Andropov worried that his agent wouldn't be able to pry the location of the bomb from the professor in time to get the bomb safely out of the hands of the Ukrainians and their western supporters. The impending Russian aggression in Ukraine over the protests had prompted him to accelerate Ms. Kovalska's training. She was a quick study and up to the task already, he felt certain.

Mykola had not heard from Oksana since mid-October when she sent him the essay and other documents. He confirmed that she was indeed an exceptional student and forwarded the documents along with his glowing reference letter to admissions.

As the semester sped onward toward Thanksgiving, he

almost forgot about Oksana. But not entirely. One morning in mid-November, when he turned on his office computer before class, he found an email from her. His heart took a thump, and he scolded himself for that. It had been over a year since Sarah, his long-term live-in girlfriend, had moved out, and he was sorely lacking in female companionship. But he was resigned to be professional and keep any feelings he had for this beautiful fellow Ukrainian at bay. Nevertheless, he eagerly opened the email:

November 15, 2013

Dear Professor Kravchenkos,

I hope you remember me from our encounter on Tatarka Beach last summer. You encouraged me to apply for a student visa, and I'm happy to tell you that I have acquired the visa and been accepted as a Studies Abroad student at YSU. Thank you for your reference letter.

Because of my accelerated program at the Language Institute, I'll start my studies at your university sooner than planned, beginning in spring semester this January. I hope I can rely on your advice in my choice of coursework in the field of political science, as you pledged during our meeting last August. I plan to register for courses in modern European history, economics, English, and the political science course that you'll be teaching. I would appreciate your feedback on these plans, and I look forward to seeing you again in the New Year.

Regards,
Oksana Kovalska

Mykola was shaken after learning she'd be coming so soon. He'd have to maintain a strictly professional teacher-student relationship for her protection as well as his. He decided to answer her with a brief, polite note:

> Dear Ms. Kovalska,
>
> I look forward to seeing you on campus next semester. I think your choice of courses is a solid beginning for your plan to major in political science. Feel free to arrange to meet with me in my office, 326 Molson Hall, if you have questions or need to further discuss your plans.
>
> Sincerely,
> Dr. Mykola Kravchenkos

As overtly coquettish as Oksana had been in Crimea, Mykola was concerned that the semester might be awkward. He hoped her summer flirtation would be replaced by serious studies once she arrived. In fact, he would insist that it would be simply that.

Meanwhile, situations were intensifying daily in Ukraine. On the night of November 30, 2013, Euromaidan protesters were violently attacked by Berkut police with stun guns and tear gas, presumably by order of Yanukovych, though he denied any part in the brutality. The revolution had escalated. Of course, Vlad was among the most avid protesters.

CHAPTER 12

Mykola dialed his mother near the end of the fall semester. "Hello, Mama, it's your long-lost son. Did you think I forgot about you?"

"Oh, Mykola! It's so good to hear from you, son. How was your trip to Ukraine this summer? Did you visit old friends?"

"Yes, I stayed with Vladyslav Domitrovich. You remember him? My old friend. We camped and fished on the Kerch Peninsula, just like in the old days."

"I'm so glad for you, Myko! Little Vlad. Such a dear boy he was. How's he doing these days?"

"Not so little anymore! He's a professor now in Simferopol, teaching sociology. We had a fantastic time catching up. We both had research to do, so we were busy in the university library when we weren't fishing. It's a good thing I went when I did. I'm sure you've heard about the terrible attacks on protesters in Ukraine. I'm afraid Vlad is very much involved.

"Yes, of course we've been keeping up with the news

from home. We have so many good friends who stayed there. They simply want their freedom from Russian puppets like Yanukovych."

"Listen, Mama, the reason I'm calling is to tell you I plan to visit you over the break. We can have some good old heart-to-hearts while I'm there."

"What wonderful news, Myko! Your Tato and Anya and I will be so happy to see you."

"How is Anya? Last I talked to her, she was busy starting an NPO in Cleveland. How's that coming along?"

"She's fine. She and I got involved in the charity program for Ukraine at our church. I guess that led to her becoming a cultural attaché in Cleveland at the Ukrainian American Friendship Institute in hopes of expanding her charity work. The NPO was created by Ukrainian American businessmen, but you're right, your sister was instrumental in getting it up and running, so we're really proud of her. She's successful and happy. That's all a mother can ask."

"I'm proud of her, too. I knew she'd have to get involved in charity. She takes after her mother in that regard. I look forward to seeing her. I'm sure she can fill me in on more about Ukraine than I've read in the news. And Tato? How is he?"

"Ah, Bronislav is well, too. He's working too hard, of course. He's been promoted to deputy manager at the plant. Quite a lot of overtime."

"I can't wait to see everyone! Give them my love. For now, I'd better say good-bye and get back to grading papers. But I plan to be there on Sviatyi Vechir, Ukrainian Christmas Eve."

"We can't wait to see you, Mykola. We'll catch up on your trip then. Good-bye for now. We love you."

"I love you too. Bye, Mama."

CHAPTER 13

The Ukrainian Orthodox faiths place the birth of Christ on Jan. 7. Only after the fall of the Soviets in '91 was Ukraine again allowed to celebrate the holiday openly, so now Ukrainians relished their new freedom. His mother, always deeply involved in the Orthodox church back home, had become just as involved in the one near New Ken. She loved this time of year when she helped decorate the church for the celebration and invited family and church members to her home for a celebration after the Christmas Eve service.

Mykola arrived to a fanfare of greetings from immediate family and extended family members who had also fled Ukraine over the years. The Balanchuks, their best friends, were there, of course, with Artemas and Galyna, home for their Christmas break. Many people from the church that he didn't know were milling about, discussing home and its plight. Christmas this year was plagued by concerns about the escalating revolution in Ukraine and the danger they feared it would lead to. Still, seeing family and friends from Ukraine boosted everyone's spirits.

Mykola was especially glad to see his cousin Denys. Denys was a year or two younger than Mykola, but they had always been close friends in Ukraine. Denys, with his degree in mechanical engineering, was also working at PPG now in research and development.

Denys had lost his father a year ago, so he was helping his mother, Larysa, Aneta's older sister, stay afloat, and with his generous salary, he was able to maintain her lifestyle as well as his own.

When there was a temporary break in the action, Mykola approached his father. "Tato, I'd like to tell you something in strictest confidence."

"By all means, son. Come into the study."

"You mustn't tell anyone. This is something you of all people should hear," said Mykola after they had closed the door and seated themselves in the study.

"Tell me, son. You know you can trust me."

"I know. But this is of monumental interest to Ukraine. And the wrong people mustn't hear it. Remember the suitcase nuclear bomb your crew lost near the Kerch Peninsula? I found it and reported it to the U.S. Embassy in Ukraine."

Bronislav was dumbfounded. "Found it? How could you find it?"

"I took a metal detector to the north side of the Peninsula, near where you said you lost it, and after spending the whole summer there, I found it a meter down in the mud, about a meter offshore. Vlad helped me. I've been determined to go look for it ever since I first heard about it as a child in Ukraine."

"Oh Myko! I don't know whether to be glad or worried. What's the embassy going to do about it?"

"I'm not sure. The agent I talked to informed U.S. Intelligence and said they'd be in touch. He seemed pleased to know the whereabouts."

"Why did you want to do this, Myko? You could have been in grave danger. Could still be in danger! Don't think for a minute we're not being surveilled."

"My dream has always been to locate that bomb. And now, with unrest in Ukraine and especially Crimea getting much worse, I knew it was now or never. Rumors are that pro-Russian separatists have been searching for the lost nuke. I think it's important for the U.S. to ensure those separatists don't find the bomb and use it against our own people. I hoped I could help."

"That's honorable, Myko, but I'm afraid for your safety. With the Euromaidan protests, I fear Russia's aggression will escalate soon. Russia has had its eye on Crimea and Ukraine, just as it did on Georgia."

"I know there's always danger, Tato." He didn't reveal the recent break-in at his office. "But I have to do what I can to help our friends back home. I'm concerned about Vlad and the other friends that we all have back there."

"Maybe you should encourage Vlad to leave Crimea. It's getting more dangerous to live there."

"I've tried to warn him, Tato. He knows I'd help him and let him live with me. But he's an activist. He's planning to move to Kyiv, so hopefully he'll escape Crimea soon."

"Maybe you should try again, Myko. Tell him we'd be happy to put up his family here for a while. The mill is always looking for more help, and I'd gladly put in a good word for Vlad's father."

"I'll tell him."

"The work you've done is admirable, son, but I worry about you. Let me know if you hear back from the embassy."

"Of course, Tato. It's too dangerous to relay the message over the phone or Internet, so I'll have to return here if I learn something."

"Yes, I understand. Please do let me know if you can, Myko."

Anya knocked and stuck her head in the door. "Myko, Tato, come help us decorate the Novorichna Jalynka." And so the conversation ended abruptly. Mykola joined the others in the living room decorating the tall fir tree while Aneta played traditional Ukrainian carols on the old upright piano. Bronislav joined the festivities as well, singing along with everyone else.

The women decorated the table with the sheaf of wheat called the "grandfather spirit," meant to honor all the ancestors. Everyone there contributed to the dinner with a myriad of favorite Ukrainian dishes. Presents were opened; wrappings littered the floor. It was a joyful celebration, and for the moment, worries over the homeland were shoved aside.

Toward midnight, the celebration wound down, and people started leaving for home or moving to their sleeping quarters. The Balanchuks offered their good-nights and hugs all around: "We'll be back at 8:00 with the pampushky," Daryna told Aneta.

"Wonderful. I'm making cheese pancakes, and Christmas eggs."

Denys's mother, Larysa, was to share Anya's room, and Denys would share Mykola's room.

When the two young men got upstairs to Mykola's room, they talked late into the night. Denys wanted to hear all about Mykola's research and his trip to Ukraine last summer, so Mykola filled him in on everything, with the exception of the part about the bomb. "Vlad and I spent most of our time in the library or fishing on Kerch Peninsula," he said.

"I wish I could get back there one day," Denys said. "I miss our excursions to Sevastopol's seaside resorts."

"I believe Russia has its eyes on the port of Sevastopol. You wouldn't want to visit now. I believe Crimea's days as part of Ukraine are numbered."

"I wish Vlad and some of my school friends would move here," Denys said. "Russian aggression is bound to get worse. With all the young people demonstrating now, Russia will only sit back so long."

"Vlad is opposed to Yanukovych since he refused to sign a trade agreement with the EU as he promised. Ukrainians are furious about the lies that brought him to power."

"And no wonder. I hope Vlad doesn't get too involved," Denys said. "From what I've read, people are being beaten and jailed by pro-Russian separatists."

"Yes, it's a tinderbox just waiting to blow, I'm afraid. By the way, Denys, I have a huge favor to ask you. A young lady I met in Ukraine is flying to Pittsburgh on January 13th on a student visa to study at Youngstown State University. Is there any chance you could pick her up at the airport and drive her to Youngstown? Our faculty meeting is that day, so I won't be able to get away. Do you think you could skip work for a few hours?"

"Of course, Myko. I haven't taken a personal day in ages. I'd be glad to. So, a young lady in your life, eh? Ver-r-r-y interesting," he said in his best Arte Johnson accent.

"Nothing like that, Denys," Mykola said, grimacing at the imitation. "She's studying English and wants to immerse herself in the language. Although she's a comely young lady, I would never get involved with a student."

"Famous last words, Myko."

CHAPTER 14

Oksana completed her final exam and dashed back to her room to finish packing. She was excited about visiting her parents in Odesa for a few weeks over Christmas but more excited about her trip to the United States. Svetlana had already left for St. Petersburg, so Oksana was alone with her thoughts. The prospect of school in the U.S., a strange country where she knew no one, was daunting at best, but she considered her assignment a duty to Ukraine, which, like her father, she viewed as still a part of Russia. Since her orders were not to reveal her actual purpose, she'd tell her parents she had to go to the U.S. to immerse herself in the English language so she could rid herself of all traces of her Ukrainian accent. That wasn't a lie, she rationalized, just not the whole truth.

She hoped that if she successfully completed her mission, her superiors would let her continue her studies in the U.S. Of course, she wouldn't reveal that hope to her parents. But with the expectation of more Russian aggression in Ukraine, the U.S. would be a safer place for her, for now anyway. Oksana welcomed having a brief respite at home to prepare herself mentally for her new life in the U.S.

She sometimes pictured Mykola in his swimsuit on the beach that day, with those limpid blue eyes, that swimmer's physique, that shock of black hair. Though Oksana had enjoyed a few trysts as a teenager, she was never in love with any of those silly boys. Here was a mature man, a professor, a strikingly handsome one, at that, and he seemed attracted to her as well. *I wonder if I might have a chance for romance. It would make the mission so much more worthwhile and enjoyable,* she thought. *After all, my assignment is to seduce him.* She chuckled at the thought.

Oksana always snapped out of these fleeting ruminations with tinges of both glee and guilt. *I mustn't let my feelings get in the way of my mission,* she told herself over and over. She was assigned to be his adversary, not his lover. She must behave.

CHAPTER 15

JANUARY 2014

Although Oksana enjoyed her visit with her family, the butterflies over her trip kept her on edge the whole time as she tried to hide her anticipation of things to come. She was relieved when the time for her trip to America crept up, and she could finally stop pretending all was well. In her anticipation, she barely slept the night before her flight. Still groggy the next morning after a few sips of black coffee, she said her good-byes to her family, possibly for a very long time.

"Please be alert, always," Olga said. "I hear there are some very bad people in the U.S."

"Don't worry, Mama. It couldn't be as rough as it is right here in Ukraine, protesters everywhere you go."

"Well, we don't go near them," Aleksander said. "Please take care of yourself, Oksana, and don't forget to write to us. Your Mama will be worried."

"I'll write often. Don't worry about me. Good-bye, Mama. Good-bye, Tato."

She was relieved when the tearful hugs and good-byes were behind her. After taking a puddle jumper to Kyiv, she boarded her fourteen-hour flight to New York. She had to rush through JFK airport to catch her flight to Pittsburgh, where Mykola's cousin, Denys, would meet her and drive her to Youngstown. Drained and jet-lagged from her trip, she was relieved to spot a young man holding up a white placard with her name written in all caps waiting for her.

"You must be Denys. Thank you for picking me up. I don't think I could survive a bus trip right now."

"Welcome to the United States. I was long overdue for a day off, anyway. Besides, my cousin invited me to meet him for lunch in Youngstown. Win win!" he said, smiling at her.

Her bags were already on the carousel when they got there, and soon she and Denys were in the car, where she promptly fell fast asleep. Denys had to wake her when they arrived on campus.

Andrei Andropov had arranged for Oksana to live in Phelps Hall, so Denys dropped her off there and carried her bags into the lobby. "Good luck with your studies," he said in parting.

"I can't thank you enough, Denys," said Oksana. "I can see why Professor Kravchenkos speaks so highly of you."

"Welcome, Oksana. I'm Alice Walsh, your House Mother," said the matronly woman at the front desk.

"I'm pleased to meet you." Oksana barely raised her eyes.

"You look worn out. Let's get you to your room, so you

can rest. You've been assigned to a double room on the third floor, which you'll share with a South African student, Annika Mbaso. She's expected later today or early tomorrow."

"Thank you, Ms. Walsh," said Oksana.

"Here are your room keys, dear. Take the elevator to the third floor and turn left. You're in Room 320. Your director at the Language Institute arranged for you to eat in the student dining hall. Here's your meal ticket and a map of campus. Here's the cafeteria," she said, pointing to the red X on the map.

"I imagine I'll just sleep for several hours."

"I understand. There's nothing you need do until a special orientation for Studies Abroad students at 10 AM tomorrow morning, here," she said, pointing to a second red X. "You have a whole day free to recover. We're so glad to have you!"

"Thank you again," said Oksana. She rolled her two large bags to the elevator and went to her room, where she plopped on her bed and kicked off her loafers. It was late afternoon when she finally awoke and found the cafeteria.

Her roommate Annika arrived the next morning. Oksana struggled to get an ear for Annika's South African English accent, which differed markedly from American English.

Annika was shy in her new surroundings, but by the time the two young women went to orientation, lunch, and dinner together, they were becoming friends, and Annika began loosening up. "The people seem nice, but everything looks and feels so different from South Africa,"

Annika said. "Have you been in this country long?"

"I just got here from Ukraine. This is all new and strange to me, too. Maybe if we stick together, we'll both adjust faster."

"I agree," said Annika. "I'm quite lost right now. I'm glad to have a friend."

"Yes, one who is also lost. We shall be lost together."

Their first weekend at Youngstown State U was spent acclimating to their new surroundings and meeting some of their neighbors in the dorm. They felt better after wandering the campus with their maps and locating where their classes would be.

Oksana's first class on Monday morning was History 310, a survey course on Post-World War II Europe. She chose this course because it would no doubt touch on the dissolution of the USSR and the emergence of the former Soviet states as newly independent countries. Associate Professor Madeline Schwartz swept breathlessly into class at 9:05, carrying a briefcase and a book bag filled with handouts for the class. She introduced herself, briefly outlined the course, passed out the syllabus, and was gone within 30 minutes. That was typical on the first day of class, Oksana soon discovered. Her first Economics 305 class at 11:00 went pretty much the same, and she was through with class meetings for the day by 11:30. She met Annika at noon in the dining hall for lunch.

"Would you care to go to a movie this afternoon?" Annika asked.

"I already have too much homework," Oksana moaned.

"On the very first day!"

"I already have homework, too. I suppose I should finish mine this afternoon too. Then maybe we can catch a movie this evening after dinner?"

"I'd like that." Their friendship was formed.

On Tuesday morning, Oksana had her English class, followed at 11:00 by her class with Professor Mykola Kravchenkos.

Mykola hoped that the reading assignments and class discussions would prompt his students to consider the diminishing role of diplomats and diplomacy around the world versus the ever-increasing military expenditures and presence of active-duty and retired generals at the highest levels of civilian decision centers of government.

As students began entering and tentatively finding seats, Mykola couldn't help keeping his eyes peeled for the one very special student he was expecting from Ukraine. And then she appeared, taking a seat in the front row, smiling at him, and crossing her legs seductively. His heart skipped a beat, but he simply nodded and said, "Ms. Kovalska." She smiled demurely and said, "Professor Kravchenkos."

Mykola went through the motions of introductions, syllabus, and the reading assignment for the next class, distracted as he was by the way Oksana raised her short skirt high on her thighs. After explaining the way their class discussions would work, he excused the class until Thursday. As the students filed out, he approached Oksana. "Ms. Kovalska, may I speak to you for a moment at my desk."

"Of course, Professor," she smiled as she followed him to the front.

"First, I want to welcome you to the U.S. How was your flight?"

"Interminable. But I think I'm finally over my jet lag."

"Good. Are you settling in OK?"

"Yes. The campus is much more beautiful than my campus back home. My roommate and I are becoming friends. And best of all, I have your class to look forward to. What's not to like?"

"Good, good. I just want to make sure we start off the semester with an understanding. I think we both enjoyed getting to know one another socially last summer. But our relationship here must remain purely professional. I am simply your professor, and you are my student. Any other way would be awkward for me, and I'm sure it would be awkward for you as well. I think it's best if we have no signs of affection, or even of knowing each other on a personal level. Do you agree?"

"I suppose so."

"Good. I'm glad we have an understanding. I'll see you on Thursday, then."

Oksana left the classroom, aware that getting close to him might be more difficult than she had anticipated. Oh, well, she could work around that. It might take longer than planned, but she was in no hurry.

When Thursday's class began, Oksana again sat in the front row but was dressed more conservatively, which pleased Mykola. After calling the roll, he instructed everyone to pull their desks into a circle, while he found a student desk for himself and pulled it into the circle as well. Oksana managed to pull her desk beside his, which rattled him somewhat. She seemed to be purposely keeping him on edge. He had begun wishing he had never befriended her in Crimea. But when they first met, he had no idea she desired to come to the U.S., let alone to Youngstown State U. He feared she would distract him the entire semester and maybe even beyond. But all he could do now was plod onward.

"I'd like to begin the semester with a general discussion of diplomacy. From your readings, I'd like to know how you think diplomacy is functioning in a general sense worldwide before we move into specific cases of bilateral and multilateral diplomacy as the semester progresses. Your textbook describes diplomacy as the skill used by nations in conducting negotiations. With wars threatened here and there, diplomacy seems to be marginalized these days. Indeed, with Russia now threatening war in Ukraine, and thousands of Ukrainians protesting, we see results of the failure of diplomacy every day. Based on your reading, do you see any examples of successful diplomacy in the world? Or lack of success? And please tell us your name before speaking so I can get to know you."

"I'm Madison, and, like, obviously authoritarians are less successful at diplomacy. I mean, North Korea is 100 percent authoritarian, and they don't even try to use diplomacy. They just dictate how things will be. Sometimes they might pretend to negotiate, but, like, they don't take it seriously. They just continue with their nuclear proliferation while their people are starving."

"My name is Oksana," piped up Oksana next. "In my country, Ukraine, once the Soviet Union collapsed, there was more need for diplomacy with the former states who suddenly had their freedom. I wasn't born yet, but my father told me that when former Soviet companies in Ukraine privatized, they began going broke. Ukrainians used diplomacy and allowed wealthy Russians to come in and buy their companies to keep them afloat. It helped my father's business to avoid going broke, but now Ukrainians are staging huge protests, unappreciative of how much Russia has helped them financially. So, I don't know if diplomacy worked in that case. Ukrainians don't seem very grateful for Russia's help."

Other students challenged Oksana's view of Russia as a great provider, so Mykola moved the conversation to more successful examples of diplomacy.

Toward the end of class, Mykola said, "I see we have various viewpoints and some very thoughtful suggestions. We'll focus on some more concrete examples of successful diplomacy, such as in the UN, the EU, NATO. We'll look at important agreements and treaties among various countries, and whether they're working. We'll also examine some examples of the failures of diplomacy, which are sadly on the rise. See your assignment sheet for Tuesday's reading assignment, when we'll begin by focusing on successes and failures of U.S. diplomacy."

He excused the class a little early and hurried to his office before Oksana could detain him. He was somewhat concerned about her apparent predilection toward Russia, but he was not yet prepared to think it through and respond to it.

CHAPTER 16

Massive political upheavals swept through Ukraine in February. News of the deaths of nearly a hundred Euro-maidan protestors by Berkut special police, as well as President Yanukovych's exile to Russia with millions of dollars from the Ukrainian coffers, plunged the country into a spiral of disarray. Ukrainian-Americans, like Mykola's sister Anya, scrambled to help the country of their birth in any way they could. Anya and her fellow board members of the Ukrainian American Friendship Institute announced an emergency conference in Cleveland from February 27th through March 1st. Anya called Mykola to urge him to attend.

"You can stay at my house, Myko. I'd really appreciate your input on what we plan. You've probably done more research than any of us. Plus, I'd love to have your moral support."

"Of course, I'll come!" Mykola said. "We've got to do everything we can to prevent more bloodshed. I'll arrange to cancel my Thursday class."

"Wonderful! I look forward to seeing you, Myko."

"Thanks. See you soon."

After he hung up, Mykola called Vlad to ask about his current situation and to implore him again to leave the country.

"Don't worry, Myko, I've already left Crimea and moved to Kyiv. I'm looking for a teaching position here."

"I'm glad to hear you've escaped Crimea. Its future looks grim."

"Yes, Russia's preparing to take over Crimea any day. Demonstrations are getting more aggressive in Sevastopol and Simferopol. The resistance here is being brutally attacked. If you can even imagine, many of Ukraine's special police forces have defected and become Russian gendarmes in Crimea! Even journalists trying to cover the demonstrations are being beaten. It looks like the Crimean Peninsula, if not all of Ukraine, will soon belong to Russia again. I'm afraid there aren't enough troops or weapons to stop them once they've made up their mind."

"Vlad, please consider coming to the U.S. while you still can. My father has invited your entire family to stay with them, and I have room for you in my apartment. I'm really worried about your safety."

"I appreciate your offer, Myko, but again, I'm simply too loyal to our brothers and sisters to leave them now. In fact, I've joined the Euromaidan Resistance in the square."

"Oh, no, Vlad. I hate to hear that you're involved in the protests, though I can't say I didn't expect it. Then I guess all I can do is continue to worry. Please don't be a hero, Vlad."

⅄

Deeply concerned over the events in Crimea and Ukraine, Mykola announced on Tuesday, "Thursday's class will be canceled." His announcement was met by lighthearted chatter and applause as students welcomed a day off. "I'm attending a conference in Cleveland on the current Ukrainian crisis. Russia is moving toward a takeover of Crimea. Your assignment for next Tuesday is to purchase or find at the library current issues of *Time* and *Newsweek* magazines to keep up with the latest on the crisis. Please bring a journal of your reading to use in discussion. I'll collect them at the end of class."

On the way to his office after class, Oksana hurried to catch up to him. "Professor Kravchenkos!"

"Yes, Miss Kovalska."

"I'm also worried about events in Ukraine," she said. "My family is still there, and I'm concerned about them. I wonder if I could ride with you to Cleveland and attend the conference?"

Mykola was disturbed that a student would make such a forward request to her professor, but it did seem logical that she'd be as concerned as he about their home country, especially with her family there. Maybe she'd sympathize more with her country if she were to become aware of the atrocities being committed there by the pro-Russian separatists with the help of the unmarked Russian troops.

"Yes, you may ride with me. I'd be happy to find you a hotel room near the conference. I'll be staying with my sister." Once he dropped Oksana off at the hotel, she'd be on her own.

"Thank you, Professor. That's kind of you. But I don't

know anything about Cleveland. Maybe you could help me a little with directions once we get there?"

"I'm sure I can help you, but I'm not familiar with Cleveland either," he said, trying not to show his impatience. "Possibly the conference will also provide some maps of the area. I'll pick you up outside your dorm at nine tomorrow." After cutting the discussion short, he excused himself and went into his office. He was in no mood for small talk.

Oksana was waiting on a bench outside her dorm with a satchel at her side when he arrived the next day. She tried to start a conversation on the way to Cleveland, but Mykola remained distant. *Well, two can act like spoiled brats*, she thought, which made for a silent trip. She fished out her phone and scrolled through her newsfeed during the ninety-minute trip. She read news of deadly attacks by police on protestors in Maidan Square. Yanukoych had fled to Kharkiv, and Turchynov was chosen as interim president of Ukraine. Ukraine was paralyzed and unstable, situations ripe for Russian intervention. She mustn't reveal her true hopes that the separatists would be victorious.

The conference was held at Wolstein Auditorium at Case Western Reserve University. Mykola had reserved Oksana a room at the Tudor Arms Hotel, about a half-mile away. "I'll help you pay for the room if you like," he said when he dropped her off.

"Thank you. I might ask you to help a little if I run short."

"Of course. The conference begins tomorrow morning at 8:00 with a coffee and breakfast reception. I'll find you there," he said, much distracted by unfolding events.

"I feel quite lost. Couldn't we meet later this evening for dinner or something?"

"OK, Oksana," he said, thinking he should probably stop being a cad. "How about I pick you up in the lobby of your hotel at 6:30? That will give us each time to get settled and give me some time to catch up with my sister before we have dinner." Oksana agreed on 6:30.

After Oksana checked in and found her room, she called Demyan Ivanov, her SVR handler at the Russian Consulate in Cleveland, to let him know she was in town and that Mykola was also here. "He won't be picking me up until 6:30, so this afternoon might be a good chance to meet. What do you think, Demyan?"

"Yes, that is a wonderful idea. I look forward to meeting you, Oksana. I've heard good things about you. It is good you are here in Cleveland. Where are you staying?"

"I'm at the Tudor Arms."

"I'll pick you up at noon in front of your hotel, and we can discuss current situations over lunch."

After Mykola dropped Oksana off, he typed Anya's address into Google Maps and drove to her house in Parma

Heights. It was a bittersweet reunion, with so much sadness in Ukraine.

"Ah, Myko, I'm so glad you could come," Anya said, hugging him. "Here, I'll take your coat. Come have some tea."

"How are you holding up, Anya? I know this convention is a huge undertaking."

"Yes, I'm beside myself, Myko. I'm living on adrenalin. Protesters at Maidan Square are being kicked, beaten, and shot by riot police. The violence is spreading beyond Kyiv, to Lviv and beyond. I worry about my friends back home."

Mykola agreed. "Yes, I'm worried about Vlad. He's right in the middle of the protests and too stubborn to leave."

"I understand. I'm afraid my best friend Ruslana will get involved in the protests, too," Anya said. "She was always the class rebel."

"I'm really proud of what you're doing, Anya. Hopefully, some activists with good ideas will attend. I'm afraid Ukraine is in grave danger. Nothing we do here can counteract an invasion."

"Yes, but maybe we can send items to support the Ukrainians who are stuck there. I don't have any false hopes of doing more."

During Mykola's visit with his sister, Demyan picked Oksana up at noon and drove her to La Dolce Vita Restaurant, where he ordered Stolichnaya and veal sausage with polenta. Oksana ate a little lighter, polo pomodoro, and a welcome glass of Riesling.

"Tell me, Oksana," said Demyan after they were served their drinks, "What brings you and Mykola to Cleveland?"

"His sister is on the board of the Ukrainian American Friendship Institute. They're having a conference at Case Western Reserve, so I asked to tag along. I'm wondering if he'll give me a chance to seduce him. So far, he's a cold fish."

"Ah, Oksana. Be patient. Some men are slow to warm. I've brought you something to help warm him up a little bit. I'll give it to you when we go back to the car."

"What is it? I don't want to drug him. I still have to be in his class after this trip, you know."

"Oh, just something to loosen him up a bit. He never needs to know. It is a tiny pill to slip in his drink to warm him up inside," he said, smiling at her. "It's not available in the U.S., but I am able to procure some from my Russian source."

"Somehow, I'll need to entice him to my room. Right now, he is despondent over the violence in Ukraine and his best friend there. I haven't been able to loosen him up at all."

"Well, then, console him. Be sympathetic. I know he lost his lover not long ago. He must be getting lonely by now. You can take advantage of his sadness."

"I'll do my best. Can you tell me any more about this mysterious Russian pill? I'd like to know what I can expect from it."

"Ah, yes. It is just a relaxation pill that will probably make him amorous and also loosen his tongue. If you accept his advances, perhaps when you are in the throes of passion, you can then begin convincing him to tell you the bomb's coordinates. But the next morning, he will forget all about what has transpired. It is perfectly safe, I assure you."

"OK, I'll have to trust you on that. I hope I'm successful."

"I have confidence you will succeed. Wear something very sexy," he said, looking her up and down. "You are a very pretty girl, you know. You will easily seduce him. Call me and let me know when you have completed your mission. It is urgent now that Russia gets the bomb back in its possession. It is rightfully ours. Ukraine failed to return it under our agreement. You will complete your mission and then call me, da?"

"Of course, Demyan. I'll let you know."

After spending the afternoon with Anya, Mykola was no less dejected than earlier. He had hoped his spirits would lift before he had to pick up Oksana for dinner. Oh, well, a promise is a promise, so he drove reluctantly to the hotel.

Oksana greeted him cheerfully in the lobby and thanked him for coming for her. "I've walked around and become a little more familiar with the area," she told him. "I've found a nice restaurant at the Intercontinental Hotel, less than half a mile away, called Table 45. Unless you want something more casual, of course."

"I'm not picky, Oksana. I hope you'll forgive me. I have a lot on my mind."

"I know. I do too, with my whole family in Ukraine. Perhaps we must put our gloom aside and try to distract ourselves for a little while. Too much grieving will make you ill, Mykola," she said, calling him by his first name for the first time since the semester began. "Some wine and good company might help you feel better."

"You're right, Oksana. I'll perk up and enjoy a glass of wine. I apologize for being preoccupied."

When they were seated, Mykola ordered a bottle of Lambrusco.

"Budmo," Oksana toasted, raising her glass to meet his.

"Budmo." They sipped, then trying to be less disagreeable, Mykola said, "Tell me about your afternoon, Oksana."

"Oh, it was pleasant. I bundled up and explored the area. I found the campus and walked around it for a while. It's not far from the hotel. Some beautiful old buildings there. I found Wolstein Hall, where your conference will be held."

"Did you get some lunch?"

"I grabbed a bite at the hotel," she lied. "Then I went back to my room for a little rest after my long walk. How about you, professor? How is your sister?"

"She's extremely busy organizing the conference. She drove me to Wolstein Hall, so I may have been there when you walked by. I was able to help them set up some of their materials. We became familiar with the control panel for their tech equipment and uploaded the digital materials for the presentations."

Oksana was pleased to see him becoming somewhat more genial over the glass of wine. When their Bolognese arrived, he poured them each another glass of wine and toasted her again.

"Memories of home," Oksana said.

"Yes, memories of a time when things were more pleasant." The wine was indeed putting them both at ease, and Oksana was finding herself more attracted to him. She thought he might also be feeling attracted to her. But she would take Demyan's advice and go slow.

When he drove her back to her hotel, they were both giddy from the wine. After she unhooked her seatbelt, she impulsively slid across the car to give him a casual peck on his cheek. At that, Mykola shocked her by putting his arm around her and pulling her to him for a brief kiss on her mouth before he suddenly pulled away and said, "Oh, Oksana. What have you done to me?" He threw his head back on the headrest.

"You're only human," she said as she gingerly stepped out of his car, smiling at him. "I'll see you tomorrow at breakfast." She would let him desire her for tonight, hoping tomorrow night things might go a step further. She realized she had a mission to fulfill, but at the same time, she couldn't help this attraction she was feeling. After all, her mission was to seduce him.

CHAPTER 17

Oksana arrived at the breakfast buffet a little early. Mykola was already there talking to a woman, so she walked over and said, "Good morning, Professor Kravchenkos."

"Oh, good morning. Miss Kovalska, this is my sister, Anya. Anya, my student, fresh from Ukraine, Oksana Kovalska."

"So nice to meet you, Oksana," said Anya, taking Oksana's hand in both her own.

"Yes, it's nice to meet you, too."

"Shall we go through the buffet line, ladies?" Mykola said.

Finding seats with other conference participants, Mykola introduced Oksana around the table, names she promptly forgot.

One woman said to Oksana, "Welcome. We need more women aboard. I understand you're also Ukrainian? Isn't it outrageous? My extended family is still there, and I'm so concerned. Do you have family there?"

Oksana nodded. "Yes, my parents are there, and also

my grandmother. They're in Odesa."

"Oh, you poor dear. You must be so worried."

Of course, Oksana didn't reveal that her father was a separatist. "Yes, it is a big concern."

Some men across the table were discussing the violence in Ukraine. "We must help the resistance. But how can we stage additional fundraisers? We can't hold a marathon or a 5K. It's too damn cold," one of the men said.

The man next to him said, "Maybe we could stage a skiing or sled riding event. Also, we can start a GoFundMe campaign. The more we get details out there, the better."

Soon, many in the group joined the conversation, discussing atrocities they'd heard about.

"The situation has been escalating rapidly since Yanukovych and his ministers fled to Russia with millions of Ukrainian hryvnia. Hard to believe the Ukrainians were so duped to vote for him in the first place."

"Yes, the Ukrainians were tricked by all the propaganda and lies," said another. "He was well-trained to be a slick politician. I'm not surprised he stole from the Ukrainians."

"And now, Putin's preparing to occupy the Crimean Peninsula," another attendee said. "You watch, that will be only the beginning. What defense do we have against Russia's huge military?"

"Some of the young separatists don't even remember when we were the Ukrainian Soviet Socialist Republic, so history is doomed to repeat itself. I'm afraid Ukraine may find itself under Putin's iron rule again."

Mykola spoke up, "I have a good friend from Simferopol who's already been displaced from Crimea. We could be getting refugees from this war and may need to offer them shelter in our own homes."

"I'd be willing to house a small family temporarily," one man said. Several others nodded in agreement.

After breakfast, the crowd, still commiserating, ambled toward the auditorium to find seats. When Thursday's session began, speakers recounted the latest atrocities. Slides of thousands of protesters in Kyiv being kicked and beaten by police were interspersed with slides of unmarked Russian soldiers moving into eastern Ukraine with tanks and artillery. Oksana was especially moved by the picture of one young woman, injured and being helped away from the Euromaidan protest, who looked like one of her high school friends. It occurred to her that many of her friends were probably among those beaten and kicked, maybe even killed, in Maidan Square.

A Peace Corps volunteer who had returned from Ukraine spoke in the first session and described some of the preparations they'd undertaken there. "This month, with war looming, the Peace Corps was forced to evacuate Ukraine," he announced at the dais. "Years ago, the Ukrainians, with help from the Peace Corps, established Cactus Forum, an NGO. They've broadened that organization to help Ukrainian students with civil engagement. They need our help more than ever now that the Peace Corps was forced to leave. Donations of any kind, food, clothing, money, are appreciated.

"Kyiv had its worst days of violence a week ago. Ninety protesters were killed in two days. Here's a video of uniformed snipers firing at young protesters holding Ukrainian flags, signs, and makeshift shields. I warn you, this is startling footage. Please look away if you'd rather not witness the bloodshed we saw. Although the Interior Ministry swore only rubber bullets were fired, steel bullets and casings were found."

The audience gasped as young protesters in the film were shot, families and friends screaming and weeping.

After a ten-minute break, the second speaker introduced himself as a program assistant at the U.S. Institute of Peace, the USIP, an organization that strengthens communication between refugees and their hosts in the West.

"We analyze strategies to manage violence and provide resources in conflict zones in Ukraine and Crimea," he said. "We welcome your organization's support and can provide you with a list of emails to add to your LISTSERV. I'll also pass this list for any volunteers who'd be willing to house immigrants. We could end up having thousands of immigrants here in the U.S."

Oksana was an eager participant in the break-out session after the first two speakers finished. She was shaken by the pictures and videos of the violence. Somehow, the grim reality of the disastrous situation had not touched her as deeply before. Bloodshed had somehow not entered her youthful, idealistic mind.

She spotted Mykola and joined the breakout group he was heading to. Each group had about a half dozen members tasked with jotting down suggestions. Some suggested handball competitions, swim meets, basketball tournaments, and even table tennis and pickleball meets, with an entrance fee and a monetary prize for the winners. Others proposed skiing, sled riding, or snowboarding competitions. Volunteers signed up to call people and write letters, proud to become activists an ocean away.

After the breakout sessions, each group shared their suggestions, with a good bit of overlap. They planned a final vote on Friday to decide which suggestions they'd get busy on first.

It was already dark when the last speaker finished, and the meeting adjourned, so Mykola agreed to drive Oksana back to her hotel. He had gotten quiet again, deep in thought.

"Mykola," began Oksana, "please forgive my familiarity, but I'm concerned by your despondency, and I feel compelled to act as a friend, not just a student. Perhaps you could join me again for a drink and some dinner? You really need to relax and rest your mind, if only as a brief respite from your sadness."

"Thanks, Oksana, but Anya has invited several out-of-town academics to a planning session this evening, so we can present a unified action plan tomorrow. I have to beg off for tonight, but maybe you could give me a rain check for tomorrow night? Hopefully, once we move forward with a concrete agenda, my mood will improve, and I'll be decent company for you."

"I understand," said Oksana, "but please don't carry this burden alone. I'm willing to share it with you as much as you'll allow. Good night, Mykola."

As Mykola watched Oksana walk toward her hotel along with several other conventioneers, he began to realize how alone he'd been lately and how welcome a little TLC might be. Especially from such a lovely young woman as Oksana, one who seemed to be interested in supplying that TLC. Maybe he could do the same for her, far away from home as she was.

He drove to Anya's house for an impromptu buffet, followed by a brainstorming session that seemed to uplift everyone's spirits. Wine and conversation flowed freely, and they managed to start a GoFundMe campaign, write a proposal to contribute funds, and send out emails to everyone on their mailing list, including the additions provided by the USIP. The sense that they were taking some action, however limited, relieved their collective sense of helplessness.

CHAPTER 18

While the conference was ongoing in Cleveland, separatists were seizing government buildings in Simferopol, Crimea, where Vlad had taught. The situation looked bleak indeed. That same day, Vlad showed the coordinates for the nuke to a few of his comrades among the resistance. He wanted the Ukrainian resistance to find the nuke before the Russians or the separatists, but also before the CIA, whom he mistrusted almost as much as the Russians. He had heard about their history of clandestine operations, including assassinations, coups, and drone strikes, and concluded that they were a rogue organization that often operated outside government channels. Soon the resistance would mount a guerilla operation to retrieve the nuke before someone else found it and used it as a dirty bomb against the protesters. Or to use it themselves against the Russians if the need became dire. They needed to act fast if they were to retrieve the nuke before Crimea fell to the Russians.

⅄

On Friday, after Anya announced some concrete plans that the group had formed Thursday night, the general mood began to improve. Instead of helplessly wringing hands, they realized that with group action, maybe they could make a difference, however slight. At least they were happier in the belief they were doing something.

Because of her youth and early influences, Oksana was perhaps the single conferee most deeply affected by the personal accounts she heard. Although she had been undergoing intensive training by the SVR in Moscow for almost two years, she had not yet become an unquestioning believer of Russia's claims on Ukraine and other former Soviet satellites. The most moving experience of the conference was seeing the anguish Mykola was feeling over events in Ukraine. She felt a strong urge to be with Mykola now, to try to help alleviate his suffering.

As the final Friday session was ending, Oksana spotted Mykola engaged in a spirited conversation with one of the attendees. When that discussion ended, she caught his eye and approached him.

"Mykola," she said, now freely calling him by his first name after their moment of intimacy on Wednesday night, "I believe you agreed to have dinner on our last night here."

"You're right, Oksana. Indeed, I did. Thanks for reminding me."

"Perhaps again at Table 45?"

"Sounds fine, Oksana. The last few days have been emotionally draining for all of us, and as you say, we need to relax. It's not too cold this evening. Would you be comfortable walking to the restaurant? I really need to stretch my legs after so much sitting."

"Yes, I need some exercise myself after these last few days."

At Mykola's request, the hostess seated them in a cozy alcove and took his order for a bottle of Lambrusco.

"We have several members volunteering to house refugees," he told Oksana. "Everyone's been generous with their time and talents. Some older women are knitting hats and gloves for the resistance; others are donating food and toiletries for Anya to send. We've got bake sales and yard sales planned, as well as pickleball and table tennis tournaments. We're even sponsoring a snowboarding contest for the youngsters. I'm feeling much better about our progress."

"Everyone seems to feel like you do. I'm sure together we can help as long as people stay this passionate."

"Oh, passion is not in short supply. I'm glad you got to see how enthusiastic Ukrainians are when it comes to saving their homeland."

CHAPTER 19

Over dinner and wine, Mykola realized how much he missed having a woman in his life. True, Oksana was not Sarah. But Oksana's life experiences and customs were indeed much more familiar to him. And Oksana seemed interested in what he was doing rather than jealous of it, as Sarah had been. Still, he must remember she was his student.

At the same time, Oksana was enjoying the attention of a mature, highly educated man. She had begun to question her mission and where her allegiance really lay. Although her father always praised Russia, doubts about the deceitful way she was recruited for the language institute in Moscow continued to trouble her, and she had begun to ask herself why she, a Ukrainian, should now be an agent of Russian counterintelligence. But the most important difference in her thinking was the presence of Mykola in her life, the effect his concerns had on her emotions, and the difficulty this was causing in her new perspective.

Neither was able to express these feelings to the other,

so they stepped back, resorted to small talk, and enjoyed each other's company and the mellowing effect of the Lambrusco.

They finished dinner with a snifter of cognac, which mellowed them even more. Mykola hailed a cab to escort Oksana to her hotel.

"Why don't you come upstairs with me and have some coffee?" she blurted when the taxi stopped outside her hotel. Against his better judgment, he agreed.

While Oksana brewed the coffee, Mykola found the blues on the tiny bedside radio. *Perfect,* Oksana thought, feeling amorous and nervous at the same time. Before settling into the small sofa, Mykola said, "Oksana, tell me more about your life in Ukraine. Do you miss it?"

Oksana said all the right words without revealing the whole truth. "Mama was not excited about sending me off to language school in Russia, but Tato reassured her until she agreed. He felt it was a much better language institute than anything we have in Ukraine."

"I suppose he's right."

"I agree. Businesses in Ukraine haven't thrived since the split. And I've always wanted to see America."

"It's also become more dangerous to live there with all the protests and demonstrations."

"It has," she agreed.

When Mykola excused himself to use the facilities, Oksana finally had her chance to drop a tiny pill into his coffee.

Suddenly feeling conflicted, guilty, and somewhat terrified at what she had just done, she slipped one into her own coffee. At this point, she was not thinking logically and was having second thoughts about completing her mission.

When Mykola returned, he took a couple of sips of his coffee and began talking about the day's meetings. Then, suddenly changing the subject, he asked, "Would you care to dance, Oksana?" He stood and reached out his hand. She took it and stood to face him. The blues music, plus the tiny pill, was putting them both in a sensuous mood, as if they had stepped out of themselves. After moving seductively to a few selections, their dancing grew slower and closer until they found themselves just standing in each other's arms, swaying rhythmically back and forth. Mykola could feel his inhibitions sliding away. They stopped moving, and she kissed him tenderly. Passionate kissing progressed to fondling and slowly removing clothing. When passion reached a crescendo, they found themselves headed for bed, any remaining clothing strewn on the floor behind them.

Neither of them had ever before experienced such unbridled passion, but Oksana knew it wasn't just the alcohol and the pills. They had grown close ever since they first saw each other on the beach in Crimea. Mykola had been trying to fight it since then, as had Oksana, but somehow, they both knew this moment was destined to happen. They had a complete loss of self-control at this point. Only Oksana knew why.

After what seemed like hours of long, slow caressing and lovemaking, they found themselves curled up together, basking in each other's warm glow.

Oksana was in a dream state of euphoria. She knew

she couldn't betray Mykola now. She also knew she wouldn't be able to fulfill her mission; she wouldn't be able to return to Moscow. She had failed. Now she'd have to seek protection as a defector. Her mind began to churn furiously. She'd have to have a new identity to protect herself from Russian retaliation. She didn't know how she could continue this relationship with Mykola, but she knew she was powerless to end it. What's more, she knew she could never get the coordinates the Russians wanted so desperately.

Mykola was having his own misgivings. How could he continue to teach Oksana fairly and objectively in class now that he was falling in love with her? What if it turned out she still sympathized with Russia? And, come to think of it, why was his head spinning?

Oksana knew she must reveal the truth to Mykola. Would he ever believe her? Forgive her? She hoped for a future with Mykola, but how could that be possible if he learned what she had been ordered to do? She lay in bed planning her explanation until she finally dozed off.

A few hours later, Mykola woke to the sun streaming in the window, his head muddled. Then he realized he had been drugged. When Oksana got up and threw on her robe, Mykola was making a pot of coffee. She walked over and put her arms around his waist from behind. "Good morning, you sexy thing," she said.

"Good morning. We need to talk," he said sharply, pouring two cups of coffee. "Please sit down." He directed her to the small glass table and sat opposite her. "Oksana,

I have had wine before. I've even had brandy before. What happened last night was not the result of wine, was it?"

"No, it wasn't," she said sheepishly, stirring sugar and cream into her cup.

"Nor was it the result of the brandy, was it Oksana?"

"No. I was going to explain this morning."

"By all means, please do," Mykola said, leaning back in his chair.

Oksana didn't know where to start. She had drugged a man and encouraged him to seduce her, originally to get the coordinates to a nuclear weapon for the Russian government. And now she was falling in love with her target. This was not going to be easy.

"You see, this all started a couple of years ago. I was given a scholarship to my school because of my ability with language. Or so I thought. In truth, my superiors were watching me as a possible asset, and also surveilling you and your research in the U.S."

"Surveilling *me*?! What is this, Oksana?"

"You see, I'm falling in love with you. This is very hard to explain."

"Well, let's get started." Mykola was getting impatient.

"Remember the day we met on the beach?"

"Go on."

"I was sent to meet you, find out where you taught, and get accepted there."

"Who sent you?"

"This is the hard part. I was sent by the SVR."

"*THE SVR?*" he nearly shouted. "All right. Start talking."

And so she tearfully told him the whole story. How she got some pills from her handler in Cleveland; how she slipped one in both their cups instead of just his; how the plan was to get the coordinates to the suitcase bomb the Russians felt sure he had; how her father was a Russian separatist and had inculcated similar sentiments in her. She said, "But Agent Andropov deceived me about the purpose of the scholarship when he recruited me. Then, after I got to know you, and you taught me more about Russia's aggression in Ukraine, I knew I couldn't carry out my mission."

"But you were willing to carry out the plan when you slipped something into my coffee, just a few hours ago! What changed your mind?"

"At the last minute, I chose to disobey my orders and drop a pill in my cup, too. Because I'm falling in love with you. I knew after all I've learned at the convention, and over dinner and wine with you, that I can't go on. And now I know I'll have to defect."

"Jesus Christ," said Mykola.

"No, try to understand, Mykola..."

"Dr. Kravchenkos," he said.

"Listen, please, Dr. Kravchenkos. Choosing not to carry out the plan...do you have any idea of the consequences? You see, now that I'm a defector and have decided not to give them the information they want, I no longer have a country or even a family. I've betrayed them all." With this, she put her head in her hands and sobbed.

Mykola was grasping the seriousness of what she had just said. If she was telling the truth (and right now, it was still a big if), then she was in a great deal of trouble. She would have to apply for asylum in the U.S. and get a new name, a new address and phone number. Mykola's anger was softening. He sat silently, his head in his hands also.

"Please say something," she said after a few minutes of silence.

"Oh, shit, Oksana," was all he could say. He sat silently, drinking his coffee for several minutes. Finally, he said, "Oksana, may I use your shower? I need to go to my sister's, think of some cockamamie excuse why I didn't show up last night, and get my stuff. I'll come back for you at 10:00. OK?"

"Yes, I'll be in the lobby," she said, rather less self-assured than last night. "Please believe how sorry I am. Think of the level of our passion last night."

"OK, Oksana. We'll talk later." He excused himself to take a quick shower, then let himself out.

CHAPTER 20

Mykola made the walk of shame back to Wolstein Hall to get his car, then drove to Anya's house.

"Well, look who's here," Anya said when he arrived. "And where might *YOU* have spent the night?" she asked with a wink.

"Oh, nothing all that exciting, Anya. I saw Oksana back to her hotel, then met some colleagues in the hotel bar for a few drinks," he lied. "I fear I overdid it just a tad and ended up bunking in their room."

"Sure, sure, whatever you say. Well, no matter. I'm just glad you're OK. You could have called, you know!"

"And wake you up? After all you've been through this week? I couldn't do that to you, Anya," he said, giving her a peck on the cheek and heading to the coffeepot.

"Well, the kitchen is still open. How about a couple of eggs before heading back?"

"Sounds marvelous."

Soon they were discussing the successes of the conference over scrambled eggs, bacon, and coffee, coffee, coffee.

Mykola was beginning to feel human again after last night. He helped Anya clean up, packed his gear, then made his exit.

"Stay in touch, Myko," Anya said as he left.

"Will do, sis. Love you." Now he just had to face Oksana for the long drive home.

Oksana sat in the lobby looking like a lost soul. He realized that, in fact, she was a lost soul. A moment of indiscretion had cost her everything. In the bargain, she had saved him his integrity. If she hadn't changed her mind, she could have destroyed his lifetime ambition to do something for his country. He was sincerely thankful for that, though he knew she would never have been able to get the coordinates from him, drugs or no drugs. It was a stupid idea. At the same time, he couldn't forgive her for her deceit. The fact that she changed her mind didn't erase the original intent.

The hour-long drive back to Youngstown was quiet, both of them deep in thought. Mykola remembered his early doubts about Oksana's allegiance to Ukraine. Those doubts were founded, which deeply disturbed him. His next step was unclear to him. Now he felt he'd been dragged into a situation where a young woman had betrayed not her own country but the country that had ordered her to engage in espionage. And that country to which she had sworn allegiance did not take lightly to defectors. Was it now his duty to involve himself in helping her establish a new home and identity? He felt quite put upon by the prospect. Surely, in the early part of a semester, he couldn't be expected to take on this added responsibility, especially by someone whose original intent was to betray him.

Meanwhile, Oksana was remembering how her future was destroyed by the emotions that led her to abandon her mission. Maybe it was because she had taken the Russian pill, causing her to feel emotions she shouldn't have allowed herself to feel. Hadn't Demyan told her just to give a pill to Mykola? Had the wine and brandy caused her to lose sight of her mission? Was it lust? Love? Mere weakness? Now, look at her. A woman without a home. Without a country or a family. Living in a country where she knew no one. Who could help her? Clearly, Mykola hated her now. Who could she turn to?

After the interminable trip to Oksana's dorm, Mykola said flatly, "I'll see you in class on Tuesday, Ms. Kovalska." As she silently stepped out of his car, she cursed herself for ever requesting he take her to Cleveland.

CHAPTER 21

2014

Mykola lost himself in preparation for class on Tuesday as he tried to put the whole sordid episode behind him. His class prep included researching the Russian occupation of Crimea, currently being undertaken. While he'd been in Cleveland over the weekend, the Russian militants had taken over the Supreme Council in Simferopol and hoisted the Russian flag. Armed separatists with aid from the Kremlin took over the seaport in Sevastopol, expelling the Ukrainian Navy and the Sea Guard, as well as taking the Sevastopol airport, with total Russian annexation of Crimea the goal. Russia was clearly breaking its 1994 pledge in signing the Budapest Memorandum: The pledge that none of the signatories would use threats or force against Ukraine in return for Ukraine's surrender of its nuclear weapons. Ukraine was to remain a sovereign state. What a lie Russia's signature was!

When he entered the classroom Tuesday morning, there sat Oksana, head bent over her textbook. She didn't look up, just quietly answered, "Here," when he called the roll.

Mykola had planned a discussion around the unfolding events in Crimea, which he began by placing the class in the familiar discussion circle. Uncharacteristically, Oksana pulled her desk to the other side of the circle. Many of the students were eager to join in the discussion and expressed their outrage at Russia's latest aggression. Oksana remained silent.

"Ms. Kovalska," Mykola finally said, "Since you're from Ukraine, surely you have some thoughts on the unfolding events in Crimea."

"Yes," she said. "I've been thinking over the weekend, and I've spent some time reading about these events. Since Russia helped my father to stay employed, I thought Russia must be the friend of Ukraine. What I'm seeing now in Crimea leaves me with doubts. I'm very confused."

Jason piped up, "I believe it's plain that the Bear is planning to rebuild the USSR, one bite at a time."

"Yes, I'm beginning to see things differently," Oksana responded. "I guess I was wrong about Russia, though many Ukrainians still sympathize with Russia. I know my father always will, and that makes me sad."

Mykola wasn't sure whether her sudden change of heart was sincere. Nevertheless, he cheered her on. "When I see a student changing her mind, I see a student opening her mind to other possibilities and testing her own deeply held principles."

The students were unusually animated, nearly everyone getting into the discussion. Everyone was concerned about Russia's growing aggression. But Oksana was finished. She remained silent throughout the rest of the class.

However, she held on to every word. She regretted how duped she had been by Andrei Andropov. She was a pawn in a chess game she didn't fully comprehend, one she couldn't escape. Always she heard from her father the exact opposite of what her classmates were saying and what the conventioneers had said. How could she ever tell her father she had doubts about his judgment? Could she ever see her family again?

Equally conflicted was Mykola. Could Oksana really be sincere? Could he ever be sure? How could he trust anyone who had lied with such heinous intent? And yet she seemed so contrite and so vulnerable. He headed back to his office after class and drowned himself in his research.

That evening at 9:00 PM in Moscow, 1:00 in the afternoon in Cleveland, Andrei Andropov called Oksana's handler on the secure line at the consulate in Cleveland to see if Oksana had been successful.

"Have you heard yet from our Oksana Kovalska?"

"Hello Andrei, the last I saw her was when I gave her the pills. She hasn't reported back yet. I'm getting a little concerned."

"Call her now and get right back to me."

"I believe she's still in school. I'll call her at 3:00. Will you be up around 11:00?"

"I'll make a point to be. Call me then."

At 3 PM, Demyan called Oksana's burner phone. "Oksana?"

"Yes, Demyan," she said, hoping her voice didn't quaver.

"I've been contacted regarding our project. I've been asked to report back on your progress."

Oksana had been trying to figure out what to say about her failure. Her heart was pounding. "I was not successful in completion yet. I must set up another meeting."

"I'll relay the message. Please don't delay any longer."

"But Sir, it is difficult to get into his confidences so quickly. I need a bit more time to warm him up a little."

"Very well. I'll be in touch." And he was gone.

Now, what was she to do? She had no plans for a second try. Her only hope was defection, but she didn't know anyone well enough to inform of her plight. She couldn't even tell her parents. The only one who was aware hated her now.

In her depressed and terrified state, she skipped class that Thursday. She also skipped class the next week. Mykola asked students if anyone had heard from her. No one had.

That afternoon, there was a knock on Mykola's office door. He opened it, half expecting to see a remorseful Oksana begging forgiveness. What he saw instead was a well-dressed businessman with a briefcase.

"My name is Charles Fritsch. May I have a word with you, Professor?"

Fearing the worst, he said, "Of course. Please come in. Has something happened?" Mykola indicated the seat beside his desk and cleared a spot for the briefcase.

"Professor, I'm from the U.S. government, here to inform you we have the coordinates you provided to our agent at the embassy in Kyiv. We haven't been able to access the area due to internal difficulties, both on our end and in Crimea."

"I hope you'll be able to access it before anyone with less admirable motivations."

"Yes, we're working toward that end. However, there's a second reason I'm here, unrelated to the first. It's about a student of yours, Oksana Kovalska."

"Oh, no! Has something happened to her?"

"Nothing has happened to her as far as we know. However, we've been surveilling her since she got a Russian visa from the SVR. We were particularly concerned when she went to a Ukrainian-American conference in Cleveland. We contacted the administration here at YSU who directed us to your office. Knowing you hold the coordinates, we easily concluded that she's a Russian asset, intent on getting the coordinates from you. We want to warn you to be extremely cautious."

"She already told me about that mission. She's changed her mind and aborted the mission, but now she's remorseful and afraid. She skipped my last three classes, so I'm concerned about her. I've been thinking a lot about what to do in this situation. If she's sincere, she'll need to defect, get a new identity and address. I don't feel it should be my responsibility to help her get it. However, I would be glad to pass on any information to her."

"I'm glad you haven't agreed to take responsibility for her. I can confirm that the Russians are watching her, and they're surveilling you as well." He handed Mykola a case with a phone inside. "If you could please hang on to this burner phone. If she agrees to defect, dial one on the speed dial to set an appointment for her, and one of our agents will set a time and place to meet with her. That will be the end of your responsibility. Is that agreeable to you?"

"Yes, I'm willing to help her that much."

"Very well, then. Good day, Professor."

⅄

After the agent left, Mykola sat alone with his thoughts. He knew he had to help Oksana this much. However, he was still conflicted by his attraction to her. If she was sincere, he would be drawn to her, yet if she was sincere, she would have to defect, and he could never see her again. If she didn't defect, not only would she be in grave danger, but he could never know whether she had been sincere.

He knew what he must do. He must go to her dorm.

"Ms. Walsh, I'm Professor Kravchenkos, Oksana Kovalska's PoliSci professor," he said at the front desk. "I'm concerned because Oksana has missed over a week of classes. She has no family in the U.S., so I feel somewhat responsible for her well-being. Could you ask her to meet me in the lobby?"

"Of course, Professor. I'll see if she's available." As a couple of coeds passed her desk, Ms. Walsh called out, "Ms. Barnes, would you ask Oksana Kovalska in 320 to come down, please? Her professor would like to speak to her in the lobby."

"Yes, ma'am."

Mykola seated himself in the lobby, where groups of students were studying, having gab fests, or giggling with boyfriends. He waited for what seemed like a long time but was, in fact, only fifteen minutes, time in which the disconsolate Oksana put a cold cloth on her swollen eyes, dabbed some foundation on her blotchy face, pulled her disheveled hair into a makeshift ponytail, and slipped on some jeans and a T-shirt. She thought she did a decent job of concealing her anguish, but when Mykola watched her walk into the lobby, he was distressed by her weight loss and pallid complexion. He stood and motioned for her to sit beside him. She sat, her head down, and hands folded in her lap.

"Oksana," he began, "I'm understandably concerned that you haven't been in class. Are you ill?"

Without raising her head, she said, "A little."

"Do you need to see a doctor?"

"No, I'm not physically ill. I'm ill from remorse. What I've done is unforgivable. I can't forgive myself, and I have nowhere to turn." She took a Kleenex from her pocket to dab her eyes.

Looking around at all the people in the lobby who seemed to have become suddenly interested in the professor and his student in the corner, Mykola said, "Oksana, you clearly cannot handle this alone. Nor can we talk openly here in the lobby. Would you agree to come have coffee with me at Starbucks?" Starbucks was the campus hangout for study, poetry jams, and meet-ups with friends.

"Yes, Professor."

"OK, Oksana, go upstairs and get a jacket, sign out, and meet me outside. I'll drive you there."

Mykola knew the gossip mill would have a field day, so he thanked Ms. Walsh and slipped out. Oksana joined him in his car shortly.

"So, Oksana," he said, not sure how to begin, "you've missed some good class discussions about the very thing you're disturbed about. I wish you'd been there."

"I can't come back, Professor. I'm too ashamed."

"Well, as you say, you have no one to turn to. Possibly

if you came to class, you'd find support among your classmates? Perhaps if you'd explain your distress to them? They all seem fond of you, and they're witnessing your change of heart."

Mykola pulled up to park near the bookstore.

"And tell them what I did in Cleveland?"

"Let's go inside and discuss it."

They ordered their coffee and found a corner table. "Oksana," Mykola began, "clearly, I'd rather you didn't discuss what transpired in Cleveland, for your sake as well as mine. It might be good, however, to explain your concerns to your classmates about what's happening in your home country. You've already alluded to it, and I'm sure they'd be sympathetic to your plight. Have you made any friends yet at YSU?"

"Just superficially. I'm too ashamed to talk to my roommate about it. Anyway, what could any of them do?"

"At least they could offer understanding, maybe help you feel less alone. It might be a good learning experience for them too. Otherwise, I guess you're just stuck hearing my advice, for what it's worth."

She raised her eyes to meet his for the first time. "What do you suggest?"

"I've thought a great deal about this for the last week. I think you're right: If you're sincere about your change of heart, you must defect. Like you, I see no other possibility. I'm afraid if you attempt to keep your given name and remain at YSU, indeed, even remain in Youngstown, you'll be a Russian target as a defector. What are your thoughts?"

"I've thought about that, too. In fact, that's all I've thought about. But where could I go? I don't know anyone but you."

"Yes, but I recently learned that the Russians are surveilling me, too, so I'm also a target. If I were to assist you with an identity change and a move, they would quickly discover your new identity and location.

"I came to discuss with you what I've learned," he continued, keeping his voice almost in a whisper. "An American CIA agent showed up at my office and confirmed that the U.S. has had its eye on you since you got your visa, apparently through the SVR. He came to warn me that you were a Russian asset."

At that, Oksana's eyes widened and darted around the room.

"You're safe for now," he continued. "Apparently, neither the U.S. nor the Russians knew that you chose to abandon your mission. I disabused the U.S. agent in that regard. He agreed that if that is true, you must defect and change your identity and location or be a Russian target. I am to call him to set up an appointment for you if that's your choice."

"That's a hard choice. Then I'd have to live in the U.S. And what could I do, all alone in the U.S?"

"It's a tough decision. If you're still loyal to Russia, you could just say you were unsuccessful in your attempt to get the coordinates. They wouldn't be happy with your incompetence, but they might allow you to come back to Russia. Of course, they would likely discipline you in some manner. You'd be at their mercy. And of course, in the U.S., as you said, you don't know anyone except casual acquaintances and classmates. Unless you contact the CIA and get a new identity, I'm afraid they'll be surveilling you as a spy. It's a difficult choice, I grant you. Do you know of any other possibilities?"

Her eyes dropped back down to her lap. "No."

"If you decide to say you simply failed in your mission, you could say that I learned of the mission so that you're going to be unable to get the coordinates. It's still a failure, but they wouldn't know the failure was your choice. And it's not really a lie because I *have* learned of your mission, and I would *never* give you the coordinates, either now or before I knew the truth."

She thought for a long time, head down, saying nothing. "But we are in love Mykola," she said finally, looking up at him with tears in her eyes. "I don't believe I can go back to Ukraine and pretend I don't love you. I can't go home and lie to my parents, who are Russian sympathizers, and I certainly can't go back to Russia. No, I must accept my fate. I can never go home. Can I ever hope that you love me, Mykola?"

"Oh, Oksana, though I care so much about you it makes my heart ache, it's way too early for either of us to use the word love. But I only want what's best for you. I planned to meet with you because I was concerned about your absences, but this visit from the agent prompted me not to wait a day longer. I urge you to decide before it's too late. Please let me know if and when you'd like me to set up an appointment with an agent to begin the process of defection."

"OK. I just need to be alone a little while right now. This is all too overwhelming."

"I understand. I guess we need to get you back to your dorm for now," Myola said as he stood to leave.

CHAPTER 22

Winter was gradually loosening its icy grip on Kyiv as the days lengthened toward the vernal equinox. March 1st marked the Russian Federation's adoption of Putin's resolution to use military force to annex Crimea. Then, in a sham and illegal election on March 16th, the majority of Crimeans "purportedly" voted to join the Russians. Unable to challenge Russia in strength, Crimea was officially annexed on March 18, 2014.

Though Vlad had been able to distract himself from these political realities by immersing himself in his teaching and research at his new university position in Kyiv, he was consumed by Ukraine's ongoing struggle to be free from Russian domination. He would no longer be the ivory-tower academic back in Simferopol. Instead, he felt himself rapidly transforming into one of the Parisiens at the barricades in *Les Miserables.* In his case, it meant joining the rebels who were fighting the Russian insurgents and pro-Russian separatists in the latest hotbed, the Donbas region of Ukraine, on the days he didn't teach.

Mykola's life, too, was transforming. He and Vlad had stayed in contact since last summer to update each other on their activities, including Mykola's casual mention of Oksana. But calling and texting seemed unsafe now. When Oksana had finally confessed her duplicity, she revealed she had a burner phone for calls with her handler that could not be traced. Mykola also had a burner phone to call Agent Mitchell at the CIA. They seemed to be leading their individual clandestine lives. Mykola decided to complicate things further and get a second burner to more safely contact Vlad and maybe even Oksana someday. Vlad already had his own burner phone for his work in the Donbas region.

As Mykola vacillated from intense passion for Oksana to some residual distrust of her, he sometimes fantasized about their future life together, conversely wondering whether she might kill him under orders from Moscow. Yin and yang in the extreme.

As the weeks passed and crocuses began to poke through the earth, finally softened by spring rains, Mykola and Oksana began to meet occasionally off campus. Oksana continued to share her thoughts and feelings about Ukraine, while Mykola began to accept that her change of heart was genuine. He continued to encourage her to contact the CIA before it was too late if her choice was to defect.

One evening, Mykola took her to a popular restaurant far off campus. "How have you been holding off your handler?" he asked over dinner.

"I keep telling him that I haven't been able to get the

coordinates from you yet. That you're cool and aloof to my advances. That I'm still working on it. I know I've been procrastinating, but this is such a huge decision. As soon as I defect, I won't be able to come talk to you anymore. Meanwhile, my Russian handler in Cleveland is getting more and more impatient with me. He told me the Russians are losing patience and want to send me home."

"I hate for you to have ended up in this situation. But I urge you to act soon, for your own safety. I don't know what I'd do if you just disappeared."

"I've been wanting to explain how I got into this situation in the first place. I want you to know that I was never a committed separatist, though I knew my father was. I was never political in the least. Early in my training in Russia, I was skeptical about what I was really being trained for, but I suppressed those doubts and did what I was told to do, rationalizing that it was what my father would want. My roommate even told me not to complain or *there could be consequences.* I never knew quite what she meant by that, though I do now. Listening to fellow Ukrainians at the conference and then hearing more about your friend Vlad opened my eyes to things I hadn't considered before."

"Well, then, that is more enlightening than anything I could teach you in class," Mykola said, taking her hand. "Like the students who raged against war in Vietnam, the pro-Georgian university protesters against the Russo-Georgian war, the Czech students who stood up to the USSR, the students in Tiananmen Square, the students in the Arab Spring, there is nothing so idealistic and courageous as a university student becoming aware of truths she hadn't considered."

"I believe you're right. At the conference, I experienced the pain of my contemporaries in the Maidan, if only vicariously. I saw a young woman in one of the slides who looked like a classmate of mine. It may even have been her. I've been having nightmares about her ever since. I'm afraid for all their safety. I can finally see that Russian aggression in Ukraine is splitting us in two. But now that I've come to this realization, I can never return to Ukraine. Ironic, isn't it?" she said.

Mykola had to refrain from taking her in his arms and hugging her. He turned his efforts to exploring the imperative for her to defect to the U.S. There was no guarantee that American authorities would even accept her defection. If they did, she would have to adopt a new identity and a new location. A new life, essentially. Oksana was apprehensive about defecting but determined to do what was right for Ukraine. Mykola saw that she was working through this process day by day, gradually breaking free from the constraints of her earlier indoctrination. As he watched her transformation, try as he might, Mykola could not put aside the fact that he was falling in love with her. Had fallen in love with her. Yet he also knew that to love her meant he had to give her up.

All he could do when he drove her back to her dorm was to implore her to make her decision soon, before she was spirited away. Before she disappeared to God knows where or what.

His doubts about Oksana grew to a whole new set of complexities. He called his closest friend Vlad the next morning to commiserate. “How is the rebellion coming?” he asked. “Are things looking any more hopeful?”

“Mykola! It’s wonderful to hear from you. Will we ever have happy moments on the beach again? I hate to report that things here are worse, not better. Crimea has been lost to Russia. The beautiful beaches of Crimea are gone. Ukraine doesn’t have the money or the numbers to fight off the invaders, so I fear it’s only a matter of time before Ukraine goes, too.”

“Oh, Vlad, I hate to hear that. Crimea is a grave loss to Ukraine.”

“It breaks my heart. Russia wanted their access to the Black Sea for ‘security purposes,’ they said. Fighting is now growing in the eastern Donbas. But tell me, Myko, how are things with you in America? What’s the latest about your friend Oksana?”

“Oksana has finally revealed her original purpose in coming here. She was a Russian asset, assigned to get the coordinates for the suitcase bomb. She was to seduce me, drug me, and convince me to give her the coordinates, which the Russians have learned I have.”

“Good God, Myko!”

“She couldn’t carry out her mission, so now her choices are to defect and stay in the U.S. with a new identity or to tell her handler she was unsuccessful and return to whatever discipline the Russians might have in store. If she stays, I won’t be able to contact her because they’re watching me, too. They could even be planning to send a new asset who is not so easily dissuaded to get the coordinates. They should know by now that I will never turn them over to anyone, no matter how persuasive.”

“Yes, now you know their game.”

"I'm also afraid for her back in Ukraine since her father is a Russian sympathizer. He could even turn her in if the Russians didn't come for her first. It's a sad situation, Vlad."

"I see," Vlad said. "What a terrible decision to make. My advice to her would be NOT to come back here. The situation is volatile, Mykola, and now that Russia is angry, I'm afraid her discipline would be lethal."

"Those are my thoughts too, but I wanted to get your opinion," Mykola said. "I've tried to encourage her to defect here in the U.S., but you've given it more urgency. But tell me, are you actively fighting?"

"The fighting continues, but no, I'm not fighting. I'm behind the lines now, helping to organize procurement and delivery of supplies to the young resistors out there risking their lives every day. The fighting of the Russians and separatists against the resistance is escalating, especially in the Donbas. I fear it will get much bloodier."

"Sometimes I feel I should be there too, helping. But then I wonder why you don't come to the U.S. It seems you could be fighting for a lost cause there."

"Oh, Myko, you know I can't leave my comrades here. There's a shortage of able-bodied and willing men. I have to help."

"I understand. Please stay in touch at this number. It's my new burner phone, just for staying in touch with you, and possibly with Oksana someday. And please stay safe, Vlad. You are too valuable in the education of our young people when this ends, so that it never happens again."

"Yes, and we pray for that day. Good-bye my dear friend."

"Good-bye and be safe. God be with you."

CHAPTER 23

MARCH 2014

After class the following Tuesday, Mykola asked Oksana to meet him at their favorite spot off campus for soup and a salad. Oksana took a bus to maintain their secrecy.

"Oksana," Mykola began after they picked up their lunch tray and took their usual corner booth, "I called Vlad and spoke to him about your situation."

"How is he?"

"Right now, he's involved in the battle against the Russian and Ukrainian separatist incursion into the Donbas. I was checking on his safety and learned that situations in Ukraine are extremely dangerous now."

"He's such a good person. I hope nothing happens to him."

"Fortunately, he's involved in procuring and delivering provisions right now instead of actively fighting. I hope he'll be all right. I've tried to bring him to the U.S., but he won't hear of leaving his comrades. When I explained your predicament to him, he suggested that you not come to

Ukraine. It's simply too dangerous while the countries are battling. His advice was that you should stay here and defect, for your own safety. Russians aren't likely to treat you kindly after you failed your mission. They're more likely to conclude that you're a traitor and execute you, or at least imprison you. I beg you not to go that route. I'm growing very fond of you, and I can't bear to even think of such horror. Please, Oksana."

"Yes," she agreed, "I am frankly afraid of either option. At least if I'm in the U.S., I won't fear as much for my life, even if I am a friendless refugee. My handler Demyan is getting extremely impatient and distrustful, so I've already decided that you can call your CIA agent to set up an appointment for me. Demyan has shared his concerns about me with Andropov and is preparing for my return."

"That was going to be my next question. I have the phone with me. Do you have any idea when you'd like to meet with the CIA?"

"The sooner the better, before my Russian handler's warning turns to action. I fear I could simply disappear from here any day."

"Tomorrow's Friday, March 28. Would that be an acceptable day for you?"

"Of course."

He pulled out the CIA flip phone, opened it, and dialed number one. The agent knew who was calling. "Yes, Professor," the agent said, "do we have a meeting day and time agreeable to your party?"

"Friday, March 28, 1 PM."

"Very well. We'll pick her up outside her residence tomorrow at 1:00. Tell her we'll collect any correspondence or burner phone she has, as well as all personal effects. Good day."

Oksana was silently sobbing when Mykola hung up.

"It's done," Mykola said. Oksana dropped her head to her hands. "He asks that you be outside your dorm at 1:00 tomorrow. You're to bring your burner phone and any correspondence, along with all your personal effects. Then it will be over. After you've gone, I'll go to the registrar's office to explain that extenuating circumstances have necessitated your leaving school. I only wish you could have continued in my class."

Oksana looked up at him, tears streaming down her cheeks. "I wish I could, too! You've taught me so much. Now what's to happen to me? I'm so afraid."

"I understand. There's bound to be fear of the unknown, but it's far preferable to the alternative, right? I'll miss you terribly, Oksana, but maybe one day we can reunite. I bought a new burner phone, so one day we can communicate, when things settle down." He took her hand in both of his as he felt his eyes tearing up.

"I suppose we should get you back to your dorm," he said.

"Oh, Mykola. Please don't take me back there now. Let me come home with you tonight."

He readily agreed, and the pair left for his apartment. Mykola and Oksana realized this could be their last night together for many years to come, if not forever.

Oksana was beginning to come to grips with what lay ahead. She felt numb as she laid her coat on a chair and sat on the couch in Mykola's living room. Mykola opened a bottle of Pinot Noir, hoping that some wine and soft music might be just the right combination for relaxing them and comforting her. He handed her a glass of wine and joined her on the couch.

"Mykola," she asked, "do you think your government will accept my intention to defect? I don't know what I can say that will convince them of my sincerity."

"Just tell them honestly what you've done, what you've told me, and why you've come to believe that it was the wrong thing to do. It's not something you should try to rehearse or memorize because CIA interrogators are trained to read body language. Trying too hard would only backfire, and then you could be prosecuted as a spy instead of being protected from the Russians for the rest of your life. So just tell the complete truth, no matter what. Don't be afraid to be emotional."

Mykola's matter-of-fact tone was stark but strangely encouraging at the same time.

"I'm pretty sure they'll also question me," he continued. "After all the discussions you and I have had, I can honestly and sincerely vouch for you. And I can back up your story, as long as you tell them the complete truth as you and I know it."

"You're the best companion and lover anyone could have," said Oksana, sliding a little closer. "You don't waste energy on handwringing, which is my first reaction."

"Oh Oksana, I've done lots of handwringing myself," he admitted.

She took a long sip of wine and moved even closer to Mykola, laying her head on his shoulder. He could smell the faint fragrance she always wore, nothing heavy, with a hint of musk. She had a certain way about her that he loved, an unexpected combination of a mature woman coupled with a youthfulness that so disarmed him. He knew he'd miss her viscerally after tonight, so he wanted to make this a night they'd both remember. He set his glass on the table, then took her glass and set it on the table too. In the dim light, they found each other's lips as Mykola wrapped his arms around her. She yielded to his caresses, encouraging him with her every seductive movement. It was a night they would long recall and one that would have to carry them through the long period of separation they both knew lay ahead.

Oksana slept fitfully, her arms wrapped around Mykola until all too soon, the sun streamed through the blinds. She woke up startled and afraid. Today was the day she would head into the unknown. Mykola took her gently in his arms and rubbed her back to calm her. They stayed like this for some time before reluctantly dragging themselves out of bed.

"Can I stay with you until it's time for me to go?" she asked, following him to the kitchen, where he started the coffee and began rustling up breakfast.

"Of course. I don't have class today, and I'd love to spend as much time as possible with you. After breakfast, we can bundle up and take a walk in the park if you like."

"Thank you, Myko. I don't want to be alone today."

"Nor do I. Here's my burner phone number," he said, handing her a slip of paper with the number on it. "I'd suggest committing it to memory and shredding the paper. If you could buy a new burner at some point, we could stay in touch someday." The thought cheered Oksana a little.

"Also, you'll need to support yourself somehow. I have a little something to get you started." He handed her an envelope with $5,000 in it.

"Oh, Myko! It's so generous!"

"I cashed in a savings bond my father bought for me when we moved to the U.S. I want you to have it to get you started. The CIA should set you up in a place to stay, but they can't do much more than that. Maybe you can find a job teaching language or possibly translating. Didn't you tell me you used to ice skate? You could possibly teach children to ice skate. Talk to your CIA agent to get some pointers. Maybe they can at least get you some interviews or suggest some places to look for a job."

Oksana flooded him with kisses and thanks. "What would I have done without you, Myko?"

"I only wish I could do more. I couldn't bear sending you off completely empty-handed. Hell, I can't bear sending you off, period."

The pair could eat little breakfast and followed that with a long meandering walk in the park that lasted all morning. Soon, they could no longer put off the inevitable. It was time for Oksana to go back to the dorm and pack. It was a tearful good-bye as they hugged and kissed in his car, shamelessly now, in front of her dorm. Oksana was prostrate with grief.

Mykola was paralyzed after she got out of the car and walked up the steps to the dorm for her things. He stayed in his parking spot and waited. He was watching when the black sedan parked in front of the dorm. He watched through blurred vision as Oksana rolled out her suitcase. He blew her a kiss, and he thought she saw him. And then she was gone. She was gone. And he could no longer stop the flow of tears. She was so young, so vulnerable. What was to happen to her now? Would she be able to survive so alone in the U.S.? After they drove off, he still sat in his parking spot for some time, his head in his hands, until he finally found the energy to drive away. He had never experienced such anguish. How would he go on?

Mykola grieved for the next few days, with no way to know where Oksana was or even who she was now. He walked into class the following Tuesday a broken man. He summoned the courage to tell students that one of their classmates was gone now. "Oksana has moved on, I'm afraid," he said, choosing not to elaborate, "but I hope we will remember her fondly." He had a brief discussion in the round and dismissed students early. Would he ever see her again?

CHAPTER 24

APRIL 2014

Vlad spent his time now overseeing supplies and munitions at the weapons cache outside Polohy to support the Ukrainian militia in the Donbas region. He had been thinking a lot about that suitcase bomb, the one he had helped Mykola find last summer. Vlad didn't necessarily want to use the dirty bomb, but in case the fighting escalated, he wanted to be prepared to respond to whatever Russia might have in store. Even if the resistance never used it, which he hoped would be the case, he thought it could be a useful deterrent if they let Russia know they had it.

He had begun relaying his thoughts to comrades, one of which, Dmytro Oliynyk, was an amateur fisherman in his spare time, at least when he wasn't fighting in the resistance.

"I have a small Rodman fishing boat docked at the Port of Henichesk," Dmytro told Vlad. "We could take it to Kerch Peninsula to retrieve the bomb."

Of course, boating in the Sea of Azov was dangerous

now, as Russians were known to be detaining Ukrainian fishermen for use on their prisoner exchange list. Consequently, Ukrainian fishermen stayed close to shore, despite the 2003 treaty establishing the Sea of Azov as common territory of both Russia and Ukraine. Russia was well known for breaching agreements.

Vlad and Dmytro began exploring possibilities for how and most importantly, when to undertake such a dangerous mission. Crimea was now under Russian control, so entering and leaving Kerch—alive, that is—posed a threat to their successful completion.

Vlad came up with the idea of making the trip on Victory Day, May 9th, the Russian holiday commemorating the surrender of Nazi Germany in 1945. Word was that, since the annexation of Crimea, this year would be the first time in 23 years that Russia would stage a huge celebration in the city of Kerch, on the very Peninsula where the bomb was located. Kerch was to be one of many locations for victory salutes to Hero Cities, Russian cities awarded for heroism during WWII. Besides the visit of Vladimir Putin himself and a military parade of Russian troops, tanks, and missiles, rumor had it that there would also be magnificent fireworks displays launched from gun turrets on the tanks over the Sea of Azov. That massive display, along with the gallons of beer, vodka, and cognac to be drunk by the thousands of expected celebrants, would be good cover for the stealthy recapture of the bomb. Vlad ran the idea past Dmytro.

Dmytro wasn't so sure. "Surrounded by so much Russian military, wouldn't we be the perfect target?" he asked Vlad. "Possibly another time would be better."

"But thousands of spectators are expected, both Russian and Crimean," Vlad said, "most of them drinking vast quantities of vodka and beer. While the fireworks have completely distracted everyone, we could quickly dig up the bomb. We'll be many kilometers west of the celebrations, and they'll all be too drunk to do anything about it anyway, or even to notice."

"Hmmm. It could work, I guess. About how much does this bomb weigh?"

"I'm guessing around 25 kg, 50 lbs. or so. Can we hoist something so heavy into the boat undetected?" asked Vlad.

"Oh, sure. The fishing crane and net can easily pick up 25 kg. How far is this bomb from shore?"

"It's only about a meter offshore. I guess we'd have to anchor a little farther out."

"I have an inflatable boat. We should be able to muscle the bomb into the inflatable."

"There we are! Problem solved."

And so a rough plan was formed. They still had a few weeks until Victory Day, time to get some others interested. Perhaps a couple of guys would agree to stay on the fishing boat to help lift the bomb.

CHAPTER 25

APRIL 2014

When Mykola returned to school the next week, he found that the vent on his door had been removed again, and his office had been broken into. Somehow, he wasn't surprised. This time, all his desk drawers had been pried open, the papers on his desk had been rifled through, and his safe had been broken into, successfully this time. The phony coordinates had been removed. The Russians would be actively looking for the bomb, but not successfully. Not with that set of fake coordinates, anyway. *Schadenfreude,* he thought smugly.

He reported the break-in to campus police, and of course, they came to interview him again and take pictures of his office.

"Do you know who might have broken in? A *second* time?"

"I can't imagine who it could be, unless it was an angry student," he fibbed. He couldn't very well tell campus police who'd broken in. Surely, the Russians knew about the defection of their asset by now. As much as he grieved for her, he was glad she had escaped.

"This is the second time they've broken into your office," said the young officer.

I'm well aware, Mykola thought but said nothing

"We're wondering why they've singled you out. You must have something of use to someone. Any idea who that could be?"

"No idea."

"Is anything you know of missing?"

"No, they didn't take anything."

"Our report from the first break-in was that the suspect had an Eastern European accent. You're from Ukraine, aren't you?"

"Yes, originally," said Mykola, trying to come up with a reasonable spur-of-the-moment excuse.

"Do you think anyone from Ukraine has it in for you?"

"I haven't lived in Ukraine since I was sixteen. I have a few school friends there, but none with any animosity that I can think of."

"Well, think about it. Let us know if you think of anyone who might want something you have."

"Of course, officer."

The campus police were not the only ones interested in the motive for the two break-ins. The department chair called Mykola into his office.

"I understand you have no knowledge of who might have broken into your office or why?"

"That's correct."

"This is serious, Professor. It is clearly not some angry student's prank, since the only suspect we have is an Eastern European, possibly from Russia or Ukraine. In addition, you recently had a sudden, unexplained departure of a Ukrainian student from your class. And now Russia has annexed Crimea and tensions are escalating. I'm afraid your Ukrainian nationality, in light of these incidents, raises security concerns. We simply cannot tolerate this in our university, especially with everything going on in Crimea. I considered letting you go but decided against it just yet. I'm afraid I'll have to place you on probation, though, Professor. I hope you understand. We simply can't afford a scandal in our college or our town. Many people here are still afraid of Russia."

"I understand. I'm sure it won't happen again." He couldn't explain why it wouldn't happen again.

"Very well. We're going to try to keep this out of the papers, but it simply must not recur, or there will have to be repercussions. You understand?"

"Yes, Sir, completely."

"You might consider exploring other employment opportunities," he added as a grim afterthought.

So now Mykola was being watched, even threatened, by the department in addition to being surveilled by Russia. If only he'd never had the childhood obsession of looking for that damn bomb. It had been nothing but trouble. He considered conducting an online search for other universities' political science departments that might be hiring. But what kind of recommendation would YSU give him now? Well, maybe if he waited long enough, it would blow over. He had to perk up immediately because he would be in the classroom in fifteen minutes. Any complaints from students about his current lethargy over losing Oksana would be just another nail in his coffin.

The Russian agent who had found the coordinates was not lethargic, however. In fact, he was ecstatic. He relayed the coordinates to the SVR, and they began to plan their retrieval of the bomb. With all the preparations for the first Victory Day celebration in 23 years going on, the SVR decided that May 9th, during the expected drunken reveling, might be the best night to retrieve the bomb and share the good news with the revelers.

CHAPTER 26

6:00 PM, FRIDAY, MAY 9

Vlad and Dmytro had driven Dmytro's crew cab with two compatriots in the back seat to the port of Henichesk, where they boarded Dmytro's fishing boat and headed south. Using minimal lights in hopes of not being detected by Russian vessels, Dmytro hugged the Arabat Spit, a long sandbar that runs along the eastern edge of Crimea. They knew that Russian ships rarely heeded the agreement to share the sea, so their trip was not without danger, despite most Russians being distracted by celebration preparations.

Meanwhile, the Russian crew of mostly young recruits onboard an artillery boat at the Port of Azov in Russia had also cast off for the Kerch Peninsula. With the coordinates the spy had stolen from the safe in Ohio, they were prepared to retrieve the suitcase bomb and return it to its rightful owner, Russia.

They chose Victory Day, hoping to retrieve the bomb, then join the celebration with great fanfare for bringing the "broken arrow" home to Russia. Plenty of vodka would be flowing, and they'd be the heroes of the night.

At the same time, the destroyer USS Donald Cook, on routine patrol in the north Black Sea near Odesa, was tasked by the CIA with recovering the lost nuke. Seal Team Bravo had regained its esprit de corps after its period of scandal—when a former NCO had been turned in by fellow Seal Team members for shooting some prisoners in Afghanistan strictly out of hate-filled rage. Of course, he had been court-martialed, removed from the team, and imprisoned. Word was that he was now undergoing psychiatric treatment after his PTSD-inspired rage. He had been replaced by the team, so Seal Team Bravo was whole again, back on track, and ready to carry out the risky operation.

Since Crimea was in Russian hands now, the recovery mission would be more difficult than if the team could have come sooner. They chose Victory Day since the Russian military would be enjoying their Bacchanalian night of revelry and less likely to spot two incoming Stealth Black Hawk helicopters in Russia's newly annexed Crimean territory. Orders were to fly two helicopters from the destroyer across southern Ukraine to the Sea of Azov, then dip south to Kerch Peninsula under cover of darkness to quickly retrieve the nuke. Once successful, they would follow the same flight path back to the destroyer. They had just boarded the helicopters and were preparing for takeoff from the helipad.

⅄

10:00 PM

Dmytro kept his eye on the GPS to learn when they were near the target coordinates, then anchored a short distance offshore. Vlad and Dmytro climbed aboard the inflatable boat and shoved off toward shore under cover of a moonless night, with fireworks popping in the distance.

Meanwhile, the Russian artillery boat was closing in on what were the false coordinates retrieved from Mykola's safe. They anchored about six kilometers east of where Vlad and Dmytro were rowing their inflatable boat. Each was unaware of the other's presence. Three young seamen boarded their similar inflatable boat with shovels and a metal detector and pushed off silently toward shore.

At the same time, Seal Team Bravo's sixteen-man platoon was en route to the Sea of Azov in two Black Hawks. They had traveled halfway without incident and would soon be turning south toward the Kerch Peninsula. When they got to the Sea of Azov, they would be in greater danger and would need to fly below Russia's radar along the Arabat Spit. This was a risky undertaking, but they believed tonight would be the best opportunity for success.

⅄

10:30 PM

Vlad put on his snorkel gear and silently slipped into the water. After digging a few short minutes, he found the bomb, exactly where he remembered it would be. He paused a moment, thinking nostalgically about when Myko and he had been at this very spot. So much had changed since then.

Dmytro helped him dig up and lift the bomb into the inflatable. Two strong young men waited with the net lowered to help lift the bomb onto the deck. Vlad and Dmytro guided it from below, fireworks sparkling in the distance. Then the men hoisted Vlad, Dmytro, and the raft aboard. Wasting no time, Dmytro started the motor, weighed anchor, and they proceeded north toward Henichesk with the missing nuke onboard, safely tied down and covered with a tarp. They had not been detected as far as they knew, but they continued to hug the Arabat Spit. They wouldn't be completely safe until they docked back in Henichesk in several hours, but they were becoming used to danger.

At the same time, the Russian seamen used a GPS app to locate the stolen coordinates and began digging as the fireworks display lighted the sky. They dug a meter down and found nothing. They dug a circumference of two meters wider and still found nothing. They used metal detectors three, four, six meters around the area, to no avail. The young seamen laughed raucously at their failure. This wasn't the first time Russia had supplied false information. Obviously, they had been tricked about the coordinates.

"Well, men, let's head to the party in Kerch and help ourselves to some of that vodka," one of them suggested. "Hear, hear," the men all chimed in, and off they sailed merrily to Kerch to join the revelry.

As fireworks lit up the moonless sky, the two Seal Team Bravo helicopters approached the area. Flying low to avoid radar, down the Crimean coast along the Arabat Spit, they noticed the dimly lit Rodman fishing vessel heading in the opposite direction. Odd, they thought, for a Russian fishing vessel to be in these dangerous waters at this time of night.

They arrived at the exact area of the coordinates that Vlad and Dmytro had just left and hovered 50 feet above as they lowered two men in snorkel gear to retrieve the bomb. The water was muddy and roiled all around the area of the coordinates, which surprised them. Something was wrong. Could the Russian fishing vessel they just saw have beaten them to the bomb?

They quickly dug down one meter, then two meters, to no avail. Unwilling to give up without an honest attempt to report back to superiors, they used metal detectors all around the area. Nothing. Concluding that the Russians had simply beaten them to the bomb, they boarded their choppers and departed north to Ukraine and back to the destroyer.

SATURDAY MORNING

Fortunately, Vlad, Dmytro, and the two other members of the resistance made it back to Henichesk without incident and loaded the bomb on the back of the crew cab. When Vlad had spotted the two helicopters overhead, he had concluded, rightly, that the CIA must have been right behind them. Gloating over their success and bone-tired after their journey, they tied the bomb down, covered it again with the tarp, and headed to the weapons cache. Four hours later, they locked the bomb in the cache and headed to their various rooms to catch up after their long night with no sleep.

Enervated as he was, Vlad had trouble falling asleep. The adrenalin rush of the mission, the fear of being spotted and detained by the Russians, and the joy finally at their success left him wide-eyed and giddy. He was already planning his strategy to let Russia learn about the dirty bomb so the Ukrainian militia could use it as a deterrent. Completely sapped of energy, he finally drifted into a sound sleep around 11 AM. He didn't wake up until 7 PM, ate two bowls of Kutya cereal, and was back in bed by 11 PM.

The Russian crew, of course, spent the night in inebriated debauchery and spent Saturday sleeping it off on the artillery boat. There'd be plenty of time to let the Russians know of their failure. Following the celebration in Kerch, no one would be in any shape to think about some wild goose chase, anyway.

⅄

Seal Team Bravo arrived back on the destroyer without incident in the early morning hours of May 10th. The CIA was not going to be pleased with their failure. The assumption, of course, was that Russia had already retrieved the bomb and carried it off in a small fishing boat. They expected the Russians to broadcast the bomb as a deterrent to the Ukrainian rebels. Hopefully, a deterrent was all they'd use it for.

Two days later, on May 12, 2014, the Donetsk and Luhansk Oblasts, on the eastern border of Ukraine, unofficially declared their independence from Ukraine. They called themselves the Donetsk People's Republic and the Luhansk People's Republic, respectively, and became Russian protectorates. With Russia's clandestine help, the separatists had beaten the resistance. Their success at independence from Ukraine had yet to be determined.

CHAPTER 27

JUNE 2014

Mykola missed Oksana profoundly. He was troubled that she would have a new name by now, and he didn't even know what it was. Nor did he have any idea what state she lived in now or what the CIA had done for her. Did they set her up in an apartment? A house? Did they help her find a job? How was she handling such complete isolation? Or, perish the thought, could they have refused protection, sent her back to whatever her fate might be in Ukraine or Russia? His grief was as real as if she had died. His only hope was that she was alive, somewhere in the U.S., and hopefully well.

His classes were going better this year, either despite or because of Oksana's absence. He hid his anguish well, and he felt his students were content and not likely to complain about him to the department. But he still had the feeling that he needed to move on, eventually. He felt lucky they hadn't immediately fired him after the second office break-in. Yet he no longer felt secure in his job. And he was so lonely. He felt completely friendless, except on the occasions that he called Vlad.

As if all that had not been distressing enough, Agent Mitchell had contacted him with the news that the bomb Mykola had reported to them was no longer at the location he'd given them. "I'm sorry to say that we believe the Russians beat us there," the agent said. "But we want to thank you for giving us the tip."

"I don't know what to say. That is disheartening news," Mykola said, discouraged that the U.S. had dragged its feet so long that the Russians got there first. Why had he ever gone to the trouble of finding the coordinates in the first place? Not only had he lost Oksana, but even the tip that he had given to the agent at the U.S. Embassy in Ukraine had failed! If he had never searched for the bomb, none of the other devastating effects would have followed.

That Saturday, he decided to touch base with Vlad to inform him about the bomb, but mostly just for a shoulder to lean on. He hoped Vlad was safe wherever he was in the Donbas region. He read that over 5,000 Ukrainians had already been killed in the war in Ukraine, many by pro-Russian separatists. He used his burner phone to call Vlad's burner at 10 AM, 6 PM in Ukraine.

"Hello, Vlad. It's so good to hear your voice," he said when Vlad answered. "How are things going in the Donbas? I read that Donetsk and Luhansk have declared independence from Ukraine."

"Oh, Mykola, Russian troops were instrumental in the takeover. Many in those regions are opposed to this new status, so we still fight for them. We've lost so many fighters and even civilians. Prom Zone Avdeyevka, the manufacturing zone at Donetsk, has become an industrial wasteland. We suffer casualties there daily. In Opytne, near the Donetsk airport, cottages and apartment buildings have been bombed; there's no electricity, gas, or water. People who couldn't escape are surviving day by day, living in bombed-out buildings with little food, with no hope for tomorrow. It's heartbreaking to see it. So many old people in Opytne are homeless and lack food and water. It's like a third-world country now.

"The Ukrainian separatists, along with massive covert Russian support, are brutal fighters," he continued, "and the equipment the U.S. sent the resistance this past year is old and inaccurate compared to the troops and heavy weapons the Russians are providing the separatists. The U.S. has supplied a great deal of money, but it's still not enough for our small army and civilian militia against Russia's huge army and modern equipment.

"Now a large contingency from Ukraine, Europe, and Russia are in Belarus discussing an agreement to end the war," he went on. "I don't trust Russia ever to adhere to any such agreement, now that they have taken Crimea, Donetsk, and Luhansk. Their appetites will never be quelled. And I don't expect we'll ever be satisfied with any agreement Ukraine signs."

"Oh, Vlad! I'm so sorry to hear all this. I worry about you all the time. Unfortunately, I called to let you know the Russians found the suitcase bomb."

"No, Mykola, I must tell you. Like you, I also recorded the bomb's coordinates that summer on Kerch Peninsula. I was afraid Russia would get to it first, so I organized a small party, and we took a comrade's fishing boat down from Henichesk. We retrieved the bomb, Mykola! It's locked away in our weapons cache now. We let the Russians know we have it and that we plan to use it if necessary."

"Good God, Vlad! I'm so relieved to know you have it! My CIA contact called to tell me the Russians got to the bomb first! Thank God he was wrong. I feel guilty now for even reporting the damn thing. It's changed all our lives."

"It wasn't you, but the Russians who changed all our lives. Don't blame yourself," Vlad said.

"How did you ever get into Russian territory?" asked Mykola.

"You should have seen us, Myko! We sailed during Victory Day celebrations in Kerch that night. We chose that night so the Russian military would be preoccupied with parades, fireworks, and especially vodka. Lots of vodka. We hugged the Arabat Spit, so we were able to slip in and out, undetected, on a small fishing boat."

"What a great plan. I learned that Seal Team Bravo chose the same night, for the same reason, but the bomb wasn't there. You must not have beaten them there by much. Such good news that my friend Vlad outsmarted them all!"

"We left just before the U.S. got there! We had just headed north with the bomb when two low-flying helicopters passed over us going south. We beat them by minutes, Myko!"

Mykola didn't let his disappointment show that the CIA hadn't gotten to the bomb first and removed it completely from the arena of fighting.

"How did you let the Russians know you have it?" he asked.

"Only the easiest and safest way," Vlad said with a chuckle. "We used the cell phones that we know the Russians are bugging to have a conversation about the bomb.

We talked about an invented location where we took the bomb, in the most uninhabited corner of the Donbas. We didn't name an exact location, though, so they have hundreds of hectares to explore."

"You're a genius, Vlad!"

"Ah, no, my friend. Just trying to stay ahead of them. But tell me how you're doing there, Mykola," said Vlad. "And how is Oksana?"

Mykola filled him in on Oksana's defection. "Your advice was good, but I miss her so much, Vlad," he said. "I don't know anything about where she is or her new name. Or even if the CIA accepted her. The wound is still open and festering, Vlad. I'm afraid I fell hopelessly in love with her."

"Oh, no, Myko, I'm so sorry. Women are dangerous!"

"Yes, I remember when I told you that. Believe me, I fought it as long as I could. But you have your own worries Vlad, and I'm afraid for your safety. I know it's no use begging you to stay out of harm's way. Be safe and be well, my dear friend."

"And you, Mykola. Take heart. Maybe things will improve one day."

On September 5, 2014, the Minsk Agreement was signed in Minsk, Belarus, implementing a ceasefire in the Donbas. Nevertheless, to no one's surprise, the fighting continued.

CHAPTER 28

A YEAR LATER
FALL 2015

After spending the summer months of 2014 and into the fall of 2015 in interviews, lie detector tests, and psychiatric examinations at CIA Headquarters in Virginia to determine if Oksana was worthy of exfiltration, she was finally given her new name, a modest bungalow in Fort Collins, Colorado, a nominal sum of money, and instructions never to use social media or to contact anyone back home. She also had to renounce her loyalty to Russia and the SVR and promise never to return to Ukraine.

Oksana Kovalska no longer existed. She was now Zoey Parker. She no longer had a family in Ukraine. She was completely and woefully alone in an unfamiliar state in an unfamiliar country. She was cautioned that not all defectors were able to tolerate a new identity in the U.S. Some defectors returned home, at which time they might be taken prisoner and sent to Siberia. Or worse. She didn't need to be told what *worse* meant.

Dozens of CIA operatives were assigned to keep track of and advise defectors for the rest of their lives. Zoey Parker had a file of invented background: a social security number, a birth certificate, school transcripts, copies of all of which were kept for her at the CIA's Secret Defector Unit. The phone number for prospective employers on job applications went directly to the Unit, where a CIA operative would answer the phone, "Human Resources," then verify her application information. Since she had studied so much English in Ukraine and later in the Yuri Gagarin Institute to eliminate any trace of a Ukrainian accent, she easily passed as an American.

Zoey Parker practiced saying her new name over and over. In her alleged life, she had been born in Torrance, California, and had majored in Slavic language and culture at UCLA. She had to leave school after two years for financial reasons, so she had not yet graduated. But her new avatar, as she labeled herself, had been interested in languages since she was a child when her teacher had read to her fourth-grade class from *My First Book of Russian Words*. Zoey had memorized all the words and had vowed to learn the Russian language when she grew up, one of the three most significant languages in the world, her teacher in Torrance had said. Now, thanks to her time at UCLA, she was fluent in both Russian and Ukrainian, despite never having visited those countries.

Zoey spent August with an operative who drilled her and tested her on these fabricated details and credentials. She visited Torrance for a couple of weeks with a CIA chaperone to learn the lay of the land. She learned where coffee shops and shopping malls were located and began memorizing the map of the town of her purported birth. She and her chaperone also spent two weeks in Los Angeles, where they toured UCLA, her alma mater, and even visited the Slavic languages department and got information on professors she had allegedly studied with. They visited the coffee shops, restaurants, and stores near campus. She painstakingly took notes, committed all the details to memory, and practiced them until she nearly believed them herself. There was no longer any danger that she would slip and let something of her old life creep in. She was well indoctrinated in her totally invented life.

Still, she ached for Mykola in her new life. She could almost feel him hugging her for the last time in front of her dorm, see him blowing a kiss as she climbed into the black sedan and was hastened into the unknown. Tears still plagued her when she remembered, just as they had fallen unchecked that day. She also missed her family and could hardly bear the fact that she could never see them again, nor could they ever know if she were alive or dead. She rued the day she had wanted to go to language school in Moscow, under a false pretense, as she had later learned.

Zoey used the money the CIA provided her to buy a used Honda Fit. She adored the cute little silver 5-speed hatchback. It reminded her of the smaller cars preferred in Ukraine. She named her Honda Fit "Rosebud," after the sled in *Citizen Kane.* The name symbolized to Oksana, as it had to Orson Welles, the mother's love. Oksana talked to Rosebud as though it were her new and only friend.

Her CIA advisor, Agent Michelle Abbott, had set up several job interviews for her. Her first had been this morning at 10:00 at the Croydon Prep School as a teacher's aide. She really liked the school and her several interviewers. The interviewers seemed impressed with her, too. The money wouldn't be great, but she still had Mykola's generous gift tucked away, and the CIA would give her an occasional stipend to keep her going. She had been informed that the jobs defectors got were usually far below their rank or ability. She'd just have to make do. The other interviews were for even more menial jobs: a convenience store clerk or selling popcorn at the movie theater, nothing remotely interesting.

Croydon Prep School was her preferred choice, so she was excited when she got their call on the burner phone the next morning inviting her back for instructions on what her new job would entail. The phone call for references that Croydon had made to the covert CIA Secret Defense Unit had gone smoothly. She was now officially a teacher's aide. Her life was finally in some order, except for pining for both Mykola and her family.

She began work after Labor Day, appropriately as a teacher's aide to the Russian language teacher, a second-generation Russian /American named Mark Sobol. He was overjoyed to have a Russian-speaking aide. At first, he just let her hand out and collect test papers and essays. Before long, she graded a set of paragraphs students had written in Russian about "The Overcoat" by Gogol. When Zoey breezed through the stack, making appropriate corrections and suggestions, Mr. Sobol was thrilled.

"Ms. Parker, I'd like you to begin helping me by grading tests and longer essays. Just a few at first," he told her one day in October. "I think you're able and ready to broaden your responsibilities. Maybe you could also meet individually with students who are having some difficulty? I think they might better relate to someone nearer their own age than to me."

"Of course, Mr. Sobol. I'd be honored."

Mr. Sobol was working on his dissertation in International Studies at Colorado State University in Fort Collins. If Ms. Parker could grade essays and tests for him, his time would be freed up to finish his dissertation sooner and move on, hopefully to a position as a university assistant professor after graduation. He hoped she might even be able to replace him in this teaching position at Croydon if she would continue her studies. Very few young adults in the U.S., or particularly in Colorado, were fluent in Russian, so this young woman was a real godsend. He couldn't believe his good fortune in finding her. He convinced her to begin taking her education courses at Colorado State.

CHAPTER 29

DECEMBER 2015

The job was going well, but by Christmas break, Zoey was getting frantic. Every day, she spoke only to Agent Abbott, her students, and Mr. Sobol. She hadn't made friends with anyone; her loneliness was palpable. She often thought about purchasing a burner phone, as Mykola had suggested. She still had the phone number of his burner memorized. She rehearsed it every night to be sure she could never forget. Her advisor had cautioned her against getting her own burner, but seeing how distraught she had become and how much weight she had lost over the past year, Agent Abbott finally approved and supplied her with another burner phone for her personal use.

"Just do not make a single call to Ukraine or Russia. Ever!" she warned.

"Oh, no, Agent Abbott, I promise. I'll just call my only friend in this country to see if he's OK," she said.

And so, a week before Christmas, she dialed Mykola's number. Her heart was pounding as it rang once, twice, three times. “Hello?” came Mykola’s distracted voice on the other end. She was speechless.

“This is Oksana,” she said finally.

Silence for a moment, and then, “OKSANA? My Oksana?!”

Tears streamed down her cheeks. She sensed he was crying, too. “Now I am Zoey,” she said.

“Zoey. My beautiful Zoey! I’ll have to practice your new name. I felt so lost not even knowing your name! It’s been so long! But how are you? Where are you? Please tell me everything! I have been drowning in anguish and worry.”

They took turns sharing everything that had transpired since Oksana was swept away. How Zoey had a small bungalow, had bought a little car, and was a teacher’s aide in a prep school in a Russian language class. How Mykola’s safe had been broken into and the fake coordinates stolen, how Vlad had retrieved the bomb and secured it in the resistance’s weapons cache.

“But I must see you! May I visit?” he asked. “I have a few weeks before I return to school. What state are you in? I don’t even know where you are.”

“I’m in Fort Collins, Colorado. If only I could say yes, Mykola. But I have to ask my advisor first to see if there’s too much risk. I’ll call you as soon as I talk to her.”

“Yes, please call me the moment you know.”

“Good-bye for now. I love you.” And she was gone.

It would be hard to wait, knowing where she was—even though it was almost as far away as you could be and still be in the U.S. She was OK. She had a new life and a new name—Zoey. He'd have to practice it so he wouldn't slip when—if—he was able to visit her. He found Fort Collins on Google Maps and looked at the photos of rocks, hills, mountains, and reservoirs. It reminded him somewhat of the port of Sevastopol where he had grown up, with the Black Sea, the hills and rocks and mountains. The port that now belonged to Russia.

Zoey called back the next day.

"Hello, Myko. I spoke to my advisor, and she said I can't have visitors yet. I'm so sorry. I dreamed last night that you had come. But I woke up alone."

"Did she say why? Or *when* you might have company?"

"No, she didn't say when. Her concern is that you're also known by the Russians. They know you found the bomb. And of course, my agent knows that I was intentionally placed in your class—by the Russians! The CIA also knows you're still being surveilled by Russia. If things cool off later, then perhaps you can visit sometime in the future."

"To be so far from Ukraine for so many years, and still held in its sway," Mykola lamented. "I feel like a watched animal, Russia's prey. One day I'll see you. I found your town on Google Maps and looked at the photos. It reminds me of Sevastopol. I'd be so happy there with you."

"Yes, it has beautiful mountains and trails. And you would make it more beautiful. We'll pray the nightmare ends one day."

CHAPTER 30

AUGUST 2016

Throughout 2015, several efforts had been made to end hostilities in Ukraine, including the Minsk Protocol. Several other agreements brokered by the French and German presidents and by the American Secretary of State had ultimately failed, following repeated violations of ceasefires on both sides. And so, the fighting dragged on into 2016, with casualties mounting and no end in sight.

Now, as the chief logistics officer for the Ukrainian militia, Vlad often had to venture into hostile areas to determine what equipment the resistance troops needed. On the night of August 7, Vlad was near the disputed Crimean border, just outside Armyansk, when the Russians and their separatist allies launched a surprise offensive, catching the Ukrainian resistance off-guard.

An artillery shell exploded near Vlad's position, and he and several of his fellow revolutionaries were hit by shrapnel. His leg bleeding badly, Vlad was thrown to the ground, gashing his head on a rock when he fell. Unable to flee and anticipating imminent capture, he handed off his burner phone to his friend, Dmytro, along with hastily conceived instructions for him to contact Mykola.

"I must stay with you Vlad," Dmytro said. "I can't leave you here like this."

"No! You have to go, Dmytro! Call Mykola. Have him call his CIA contact and tell them to call my burner for the bomb's location. You must give the location to the CIA. Maybe they can use it as a bargaining chip to get some prisoners released. It's our only hope."

The Russians were closing in on the wounded Vlad. "GO! Get out of here!" he said to Dmytro. And so Dmytro ran, tears welling up over abandoning his friend.

Although Dmytro escaped, Vlad was captured along with several other opposition troops and taken to a prisoner of war camp near Luhansk, close to the border with Russia. Fortunately, the troops who were captured along with Vlad were able to tie a tourniquet around his leg to stanch the bleeding during transport. Vlad slipped in and out of consciousness, but despite bumping and jostling painfully through rough terrain and bombed-out roads, he survived the trip.

Enough bandages and medical supplies were available at the camp to patch up the wounded. After a few days' convalescence, Vlad was eager to get up from his cot. Someone found him a strong limb in the fenced prison yard to use as a cane, so he could walk a short distance and gradually build up his strength. His headaches were blinding, though, and it was determined he had a concussion from the fall.

This skirmish, along with another on the following day, triggered buildups on both sides of the disputed border. Putin canceled planned negotiations for a settlement, which was to have taken place in China in January between Russia, Ukraine, France, and Germany. The fighting would rage on.

Traveling on foot, along with a few other fortunate escapees, Dmytro had made his way back to a fortified Ukrainian position to report the incident. Finding some privacy in the woods surrounding the headquarters, he selected speed-dial number 1, Mykola's burner number. Mykola picked up and said, "Hello, Vlad. Great to hear from you."

"Hello, Mykola? I'm friends with Vlad. My name is Dmytro Oliynyk," Dmytro said in Ukrainian. "He wanted me to call to tell you he's been captured by the Russian separatists and taken to a prison camp somewhere in the Donbas."

"Oh, no! Is he OK?"

"He was wounded by shrapnel, but his injuries did not seem terribly serious," Dmytro fibbed, remembering the spurting blood he had seen. "He insisted I leave him so I could contact you. He handed me his burner phone before the Russians could confiscate it, so you won't be able to get in touch with him. He asked me to have you call your CIA contact, in hopes they could use the bomb as a bargaining chip for the release of Ukrainian prisoners, including Vlad. He said you would know how to proceed with this plan. You can ask the CIA to contact me at this number since I know the exact location of the bomb. I was with Vlad when we retrieved it and when we concealed it."

"Oh my God," said Mykola. "I'm glad you have the

bomb, but I hate to hear this news of Vlad. I've been so worried. May I contact you at this number?"

"Yes, I'll be his proxy for now. Call anytime. I'm your friend now, too."

"Thank you, Dmytro. If you get any updates on Vlad's condition, would you please call me?"

"Yes, if I hear anything, I'll be sure to let you know."

"Thank you. Vlad's plan sounds good. If the bomb becomes a bargaining chip for his release, then I'll feel a little less guilty. Thanks for contacting me. And please, be careful! Now I will worry about you, too."

After the call, Dmytro entered the headquarters for his debriefing on the current situation near Armyansk.

CHAPTER 31

AUGUST 2016

Mykola hung up and called his CIA contact. "Agent Mitchell, this is Mykola Kravchenkos. I just learned that my friend Vlad in Ukraine has been wounded and taken prisoner. I also learned that the Russians did not get the nuke. The resistance has it. Vlad's friend Dmytro knows the bomb's location and wants you to call him on his burner. They're hoping you can use the bomb as a bargaining chip to release prisoners."

"Well, that is good news. Did he give any idea where the bomb is now?"

"It's locked in a weapons cache somewhere in Ukraine. Dmytro knows exactly where."

"What's Dmytro's last name? And have you known him long?"

"Dmytro Oliynyk." He spelled the first and last names for the agent. "I just met him on Vlad's burner phone, but I've known Vlad since primary school. He helped me find the bomb. You can trust him, and Dmytro too, I'm sure.

Dmytro helped Vlad retrieve and secure the bomb."

"Yes, I'm sure we can trust him. It's just that we have to know exactly who we're dealing with. You understand."

"Of course." He gave the agent Vlad's phone number.

"I'll let you know when we learn anything. We'll notify the NTI, the Nuclear Threat Initiative. Their Cooperative Threat Reduction Program will handle it. I imagine they'll try to retrieve the bomb, dismantle it, and use it as a bargaining chip. Thanks for the info, Mykola."

"Please let me know if it can be used for a prisoner swap. I'm extremely worried about Vlad."

"Yes. we'll be in touch."

Mykola continued his waiting game. Waiting to see when he could visit Zoey. Waiting to see if Vlad would recover and be released from prison camp. Waiting to see if the NTI could recover the bomb. The semester inched imperceptibly along, and he still knew nothing.

That night, he called Zoey. After he filled her in on the trouble Vlad was in, and after Zoey filled him in on her lonely TV dinner in front of *Kevin Can Wait*, he changed the subject to more personal concerns.

"But Zoey, you mustn't wait for me. If opportunities arise for your happiness without me, please don't hesitate to accept them. This has all been my fault, and I don't want you to continue to suffer for my errors."

"Oh, Myko, I'll always be waiting for you. There could

never be anyone else. My God, Myko, I gave up my country for you."

"I hope I can visit soon. I'll be yearning for you until we meet again. Good-bye, my love."

CHAPTER 32

DECEMBER 2016

The semester crept slowly but persistently toward winter break. One cold December day, Zoey's burner phone, which so seldom rang, startled her. She hastened to answer it, thinking it might be Mykola. Instead, it was the other burner phone, the one belonging to her CIA contact. "Zoey, I must see you tomorrow morning," Agent Abbott said. "I'll meet you at your house at 8 AM. I have some urgent news."

At 7:55 the next morning, a rap on the door brought Zoey quickly to her feet from where she sat in anticipation.

"Come in," she said. "Please, have a seat. I've just made coffee. How do you take it?"

"Two sugars and cream, please," Agent Abbott said, finding a seat on the couch.

Zoey brought the tray and set it on the coffee table. "Please tell me, what's so urgent? I barely slept a wink."

Stirring cream into her coffee, Agent Abbott said, "Zoey, I'm afraid I have bad news. We have intelligence that Russian spies are actively looking for you to return you to Russia as a traitor."

"Oh, my God!" she said. "But my new identity? Have they discovered my location? What can I do?" The questions spewed forth before Agent Abbott could speak.

"Calm down, Zoey," she said. "They don't know where you are yet. We have time because they're searching far east of Colorado for now. Our biggest concern is that CCTV is becoming more widespread, so they could spot you anywhere. There are thirty million plus surveillance cameras in the U.S. now. The Russians walk among us as Americans, so they could easily gain access to cameras anyplace you frequent. We have evidence that spies are hacking into monitors. And they're intent on finding you, now that they know you've disappeared."

"Is there anything we can do?" Zoey asked.

"The only sure deterrent is disguise. You'll need to change your hair completely, color and length. You must become a short-haired brunette, I'm afraid."

"Could I let it grow back out if the threat is over someday?"

"Perhaps. But, sometimes, years later, they still locate a defector. They're persistent. It just depends on how important you are to them. But that's not all. You'll also need to take a more drastic step."

Zoey gasped, "Not surgery?"

"I'm afraid so. I hate to suggest doing it to your beautiful face," Agent Abbott said. "But, with your consent, we should try minimal surgery. Usually, with rhinoplasty, along with microdermabrasion, the face will be changed enough to avoid detection by facial recognition software. Microdermabrasion is simply a chemical peel, which, along with a skin lightening product, can lighten your skin enough that the software will reject it. Alone, lighter skin might not be enough. Rhinoplasty to change the shape of your nose would then make your face less likely to register on the software."

"But how would you change my nose?" she asked.

"We'd have you look at pictures and pick out just the look you want. You can choose a model's nose if you like," said Agent Abbott, trying to cheer her. "I'm afraid it's our only hope. With Russia's recent technology, our attempts at going undercover have gotten much more complex."

"Do you think I'll have to do any more than that?"

"After your face heals completely, we'll try our facial recognition software to see if you've fooled it. There are some other steps we could take if necessary, such as making your lips a little fuller. I know it's a huge inconvenience, but it could be the only way for you to stay in the country and be safe."

"How much school would I have to miss?"

"Probably about three weeks, maybe less. If we act fast, we can get it done during your Christmas break, plus possibly one more week. We have an appointment for you to meet a specialist at Fitzsimons Army Hospital in Aurora this Friday, the 16th," she continued. "You shouldn't have to miss more than a few days after the New Year, if that."

Zoey was silent.

"Do you need a day to think about it?"

"No. I'll do it. I don't see any other choice," she said glumly.

"I'm relieved. I'd be devastated if the Russians located you, Zoey. Rest assured, this is the right decision. I'll pick you up at 12:30 Friday."

"Yes, ma'am. I'll be ready."

Agent Abbott let herself out.

Friday afternoon, the agent drove Zoey to Aurora for the appointment. Dr. Brumfield greeted them with a smile in the exam room.

"I understand you'd like a little different look," he said cheerfully.

"*Little* is the operative word," Zoey said. "Possibly a slight change to my nose?"

"Of course. Ms. Abbott already filled me in, so I've brought in some choices for an even more beautiful nose than the one you have now."

Zoey reluctantly took the notebook from him and leafed through it, bewildered by so many choices.

"I realize there are too many to choose from with a quick look," Dr. Brumfield said. "If you just pick one or two from each category, we'll use 3D imagery to show you how you'd look. We can work from there."

And so, with the help of Agent Abbott and the doctor, Zoey picked out a new look that she thought might even enhance her appearance. Dr. Brumfield then explained the procedure and what to expect throughout. He would make incisions inside her nose, so there would be no visible incisions or scars. She would wear a splint for a week, after which she'd still have some bruising around her eyes and nose. After two weeks, she could hide any residual bruising with some cover-up and return to school. Some swelling would remain, but it should not be detectable during the month or two it would take before she would realize her completed new look.

"Should I get microdermabrasion before or after surgery?" Zoey asked.

"Sometimes there will be some dry, flaky skin after rhinoplasty. I'd suggest the microdermabrasion about eight weeks later."

"As I've mentioned, Doctor," said Agent Abbott, "we need the surgery ASAP."

"I'm aware. We have her scheduled for surgery Monday morning, December 19, at 10 AM. It's outpatient surgery, so she'll go home after a short time in recovery.

And so Zoey would officially become Zoey in every way now, a young woman who no longer even looked like Oksana.

Fifteen hundred miles away, what may as well have been a world away, Mykola planned another Orthodox Christmas visit to his family. Along with their traditional Ukrainian meal, they would eat braided kolach bread, the three braids signifying the Holy Trinity.

When he arrived on January 5th, everyone was in reasonably good spirits, considering the ongoing fighting back home. Except Mykola. He tried not to show the worries that plagued him, but his mother took him aside. She knew something was not right with him.

"Why so glum, Myko? Your family's here together, everyone is cheerful. And you look like you lost your last friend. What's wrong, son?"

"Oh, Mama," he said, "you're right. I have some concerns on my mind. I'm afraid I shouldn't have come."

"Don't say that, Myko! Please share your concerns

with your family. We want to support you, but how can we when we don't know what's bothering you?"

"Only that my friend Vlad was wounded and is in a prison camp. He's much on my mind."

"Oh no. I'm sorry, Myko. We'll all pray for your friend Vlad."

Mykola didn't share any more than that with his mother, but later that afternoon, when guests had scattered into smaller groups, he took Denys into the office and confided in him. Denys knew Oksana, but that Mykola had fallen in love with her and that she had defected was news to him. Mykola also shared concerns about the bomb and his hope that the NTI would gain control of it. And, of course, he told Denys of his worries for Vlad's safety. His burdens were heavy.

"I'm hoping that one day Oksana and I are reunited," he told Denys. "But for now, I'm being surveilled by Russia, so her advisor is barring a visit. Please, please, Denys, I'm entrusting you with this top-secret information. Promise me you won't repeat any of it. Our lives literally depend on secrecy."

"Of course, I promise. But do you think it's wise *ever* to visit her? It sounds risky, not only for you, but for her. If she's in hiding, a visit from you could tip the Russians off to her whereabouts. As long as war continues in Ukraine, Russians will be interested in the defector's whereabouts. Can you at least speak to her on the phone for now?"

"Yes, we both have burner phones. At least I know where she is, that she's safe, has a job, a place to live. But I miss seeing her so much, Denys, and she tells me how lonely she is, alone in a new country."

"Of course, Myko. Try to be grateful that she's been accepted by the CIA as a defector. They could have accused her of being a spy and imprisoned her! Try to look at it that way, Myko. Chin up, eh? Things will improve."

Venting to Denys helped, and to placate his mother, he pasted on a smile and ended everyone's worries for the time being.

Ever true to his family, Denys never spoke again of the secret he'd been entrusted with.

CHAPTER 33

JANUARY 2017

To all appearances, Oleg Vasiliev was an upstanding member of the Cleveland community, a prominent parishioner of St. Sergius Russian Orthodox Cathedral, and the proprietor of Oleg's, a popular Slavic restaurant in Mayfield Heights. No one in Cleveland knew Oleg was a sleeper agent of Russia to be activated only for a specific mission and otherwise not an active agent at all. The SVR was able to successfully get Oleg into the United States on an investor visa in 1992, following the Soviet dissolution. After getting his green card in 1995, he went on to become an American citizen in 2006, and his cover was thereby secured.

Oleg was assigned the mission of capturing Oksana and sending her back to Russia for prosecution as a traitor. He was not to execute her himself but rather to have her returned to be interrogated by the SVR in hopes of getting whatever intelligence she might have obtained from her Ukrainian-American cohorts while in the U.S. Oleg knew that once they were finished with her questioning, she would be eliminated.

Oleg's handler, Demyan Ivanov, provided him with a laptop loaded with the latest facial recognition software that the Russians had been developing, along with recently obtained photos of Oksana. Briefed on Oksana's defection, Oleg was to follow Mykola on any out-of-town trips in hopes that Mykola would lead him to his prey. Oleg was also notified that two other members of the sleeper cell were also activated to assist in the mission: Marina, a software designer in Cincinnati, and Mischa, a martial arts instructor in Columbus. Marina would use her computer skills to hack into nearby CCTV systems and load the facial recognition software, while Mischa's skills would be useful for kidnapping Oksana and quietly removing her to Moscow. On command from their handler at the consulate, the trio of agents would rendezvous in the city where Mykola would unwittingly lead them to capture their prey. Of course, Mykola would also be monitored more closely in Youngstown.

Meanwhile, Mykola had been chafing under the CIA's restrictions on contact with Oksana. As spring break approached, Mykola risked getting in touch with Zoey via their burner phones.

"Zoey, this is Mykola. Are you all right? Can you talk now?"

"Yes, Mykola, I'm OK. I miss you and I want to see you. My advisor said it's still not safe to meet, but I'm going crazy."

"Zoey, I know we're not supposed to get together yet, but this separation is driving me nuts, too! It's already gone on for years. I can't take much more. Let's arrange to meet somewhere near your home, but not so close as to attract suspicion. Could you drive to Estes Park on Saturday, April 9th, and meet me in the bar at the Ridgeline Hotel around three? I've already made reservations there for the weekend."

"Myko," said Zoey, "I'm scared to risk losing the CIA's help. Are you sure we'll be safe?"

"Honestly, Zoey, I'm not sure of anything anymore, except that I love you and want to be with you. Are you willing to take the chance to meet?"

"Yes, Mykola," said Zoey. "I'll meet you there and all will be well."

"Wonderful. You've made my day. So long for a little while, then, Zoey."

Neither was sure that all would be well.

Oleg, carrying out orders to track Mykola's movements, knew when Mykola bought his plane ticket to Denver. Oleg's fellow agent Marina detected the transaction, as well as the car rental reservation, and promptly reported them to the team members. Oleg booked round-trip seats on the same flights as well as a rental car from the same agency Mykola used. He would follow Mykola's movement in hopes he would lead them to the defector.

CHAPTER 34

APRIL 2017

At last, April 9th arrived. Since the Big Thompson River, which carries snowmelt down the canyon, had broken the dam at Lake Estes several years earlier and roared down the canyon, the two-lane road through the majestic granite-walled canyon would be closed until road crews rebuilt the damaged roads and bridges through the canyon. The construction and detours doubled the time for Zoey's trip. Fortunately, Mr. Sobol alerted her to the closure and showed her the circuitous route she'd have to take, south, then west, then north to Estes Park. She told him she was meeting a cousin from Torrance there.

Meanwhile, Mykola picked up his rental car at Denver International and made his way north to Estes Park. Thoughts of seeing Zoey so occupied his mind that he never noticed the agent a safe distance behind him.

Zoey was worried that Myko might not like her changed appearance. She knew Agent Abbott would be angry if she found out where she'd gone. But it had been so long, and her loneliness was leading her into a deep depression that she could no longer ignore.

A gust of cold April wind caught her in the hotel parking lot and almost caused her to lose her balance. When she was safely inside, she found the ladies' room, took off her wool cap, and straightened her brunette pixie haircut. She touched up her lipstick, smoothed her dress, and went to the restaurant. Mykola hadn't arrived, so she found a hi-top table by the window. She was glad she had preceded him. She hadn't told him about the short haircut, the narrower nose, or the lighter skin, and she wanted to look "just so" when he arrived.

The waiter stepped over to get her drink order, and as he walked away, Zoey saw Mykola just entering. She could so easily have dashed over and thrown herself in his arms, but she sat stoically as his gaze searched the bar for her. Grinning, she finally waved at him. She had fooled him! He walked over warily, then finally recognized her.

"Is this really my Zoey?" he asked as she stood and folded herself into his arms.

"Yes, Myko, it's me! I have much to tell you!"

"I can see that!" He was smiling as he held her at arm's length to look at her.

"I wanted to surprise you. Do you like my new look?"

"You are as beautiful as ever. But I wouldn't have recognized you. Besides your new hairdo, you've lost so much weight."

"Agent Abbott made me change my appearance to fool the Russian facial recognition software. I've darkened my hair, changed my nose, and lightened my skin. The weight loss is just from the loneliness since we parted. I've had to force myself to eat. I'm happy I fooled you. Maybe I'll fool the Russians too."

"But what happened to your beautiful blue eyes?"

"It's just brown contact lenses. They're still blue underneath."

Mykola pulled his chair closer to hers. When the waiter brought Zoey's Pinot Grigio, Mykola said, "I'll try a glass of that Latitude 105 ale I see lining the wall over there."

"Yes, sir," the waiter said.

"I can't keep my eyes off you!" he said to Zoey after the waiter left to pour his ale. "You are beautiful in a new way. A mysterious, exotic woman. Alluring. A woman to be properly seduced, and I'm just the man to do the seducing," he said, squeezing her thigh under the table. "I think after our drinks, we should go up to our room. We shouldn't be out in the open, and we have so little time. Let's just order a small dinner from room service."

"Anything, as long as it's with you."

"Tell me about yourself, Zoey. How's your job?" Mykola asked, settling back to earth. "Are you enjoying teaching?"

"I'm not really teaching, just an aide. I grade papers, interact with students who need extra help. But when Mr. Sobol finishes his dissertation, he'll move on to a university position, and he's going to recommend to the administration that I replace him when he leaves! I'm taking education courses so that I'll be ready to take over."

"That's wonderful news! I'm so proud of you. Do you think you'll enjoy teaching?"

"I do enjoy teaching. Mr. Sobol lets me conduct class

sometimes. He's teaching me how to prepare lesson plans and keep gradebooks. Since he's nearly completed his PhD, he's able to be my advisor as a student teacher, so I'll be finished with that requirement. He's preparing me to take over the class on day one. I just hope the administration agrees with his recommendation."

"How could they not? I'm sure the students love you. How have they taken to your new look?"

"They give me compliments on my hair, but I don't think they've noticed anything else."

Mykola caressed her cheek and said, "Your skin feels like silk and looks like a peach. I don't know if you realize how gorgeous you are. I'm dying to kiss you. But not here."

"I'm glad you approve," she said. "But as for the students, they are decidedly unobservant except among their peers."

"They must be! You've grown from an innocent child to a sensuous woman, and I find you stunning! I'd like to explore the new Zoey in the room. Shall we go up? Besides wanting to seduce you, I want to get you out of public view. Do you have luggage in your car?"

"I've brought all I need in this tote bag," she said, nodding toward the bag hanging from the back of her chair.

"Good. I've checked in already, so let's go get settled in. Our time together is way too short." They swallowed one last sip of their drinks and headed to the elevator.

CHAPTER 35

APRIL 2017

As the door clicked shut behind them, Zoey melted in Mykola's arms. When they dragged themselves out of each other's arms, they ordered champagne and one order of veal parmesan to split; neither of them was able to eat more than a few bites. They couldn't keep their hands off each other as they sipped their champagne and nuzzled.

"Oh, Zoey, what have you done to me?" Mykola said. "And what are we going to do now?"

"I don't know, Myko," Zoey said. "I'm a prisoner in a strange country. You're my only hope, yet I can't be with you."

"Are you sorry you defected? It was a consequential decision, and now you're paying a steep price. I hate seeing you so despondent."

"No, it would be much worse if I hadn't defected. I couldn't go through with the horrible assignment that I felt coerced into accepting. That left only one option. If I had gone home, defeated, it would have been a much worse sort of prison: an actual prison or even death. But now, what can we do?"

"All I can come up with is to wait until they give up on surveilling us. It could take years, I suppose. And of course, you don't have to wait for me. If you meet someone who could make you happy, you'd be released from the pain you're experiencing now."

"Oh, never say that! You're the reason I had to defect! I could never have completed my mission. How did I ever think I'd be capable? I fell hopelessly in love."

"Even in my grouchy moods?"

"Even when you're grouchy, silly," she said, caressing his cheek.

"I'm sorry. I was trying hard NOT to fall in love with you. I had to be strict, keep a professional teacher-student relationship. But you're not my student anymore! Now my heart can overflow with love for you."

Zoey clung to him as though she could never let go. The night was for caressing, snuggling, intimacy, but certainly not for sleeping.

Finally, near dawn, they slept briefly. They woke, wrapped in each other's arms, as the sun just began to peep through the shade. Today was the day they would return to their lives apart from one another.

"Oh, my beautiful Zoey, I don't think I can bear this separation much longer," Mykola said, lying spread eagle on the bed. "I've got to figure out a way to join you here in Colorado. But how to do that without putting you in grave danger? My brain is in such turmoil."

"I know, Myko. Some days I don't think I can go on."

"I keep telling myself that we have to just take one step at a time, one day at a time. We're strong enough to get through this, and we'll be together one day, I promise you. It seems impossible, but if you can just concentrate on your studies and teaching, the time will pass.

"For now, though," he continued, putting a smile on his face, "I guess we need to perk up, get dressed, and go downstairs for some breakfast before we have to go our separate ways." Zoey moaned, but she obeyed.

Hungry after very little dinner, Zoey filled her plate at the buffet and went to the same table where they met yesterday. While they munched on their omelets, bacon, and muffins, Zoey told Mykola of the roundabout route she had taken to get to Estes Park. "Now I have to travel south before I can travel north," she said with a laugh.

"I'm sorry. If I'd known, I'd have thought of a different meeting place," Mykola said. "I'm traveling south too, to Denver. Follow me, flash your lights just before your turn, and we can stop for one last hug when we part ways."

"One last moment to look forward to," she said.

Zoey kept her eye on other breakfasters filing through the buffet line and finding tables. One lone man caught her eye. He seemed to notice them as he walked by their table. He sat at a table near them and took out his phone. Zoey noticed that the phone in his left hand faced toward them. He would take a sip of coffee then look back at the phone.

"Don't look now, but I think we're being watched," she told Mykola quietly. "A man might be taking my picture with his phone. It's aimed in this direction, and he's reading it—or pretending to."

"Let's get out of here," Mykola said, rising. They went

straight to check out, Zoey carrying her last piece of muffin. Then Mykola escorted her to her car. "This has to be quicker than I planned," he said, hugging her one last time, and got in his own rental.

Oleg exited the hotel behind them and got into his vehicle. Mykola didn't notice him, but Zoey noted Oleg's blue Subaru. When Oleg also turned south, she phoned Mykola to alert him.

"I believe the man in the restaurant is following us," she said. "He's behind me."

"I'll watch him. Hopefully, he's just taking the same route I am to the airport," Mykola said, trying to calm her. "I guess we'd better forgo that last hug until next time. Call when we get close to your turnoff."

Oleg, close on their tail, had taken several pictures of Zoey at breakfast and sent them to Marina while he drove. "Run thru software ASAP," he texted.

Within minutes, she texted back, "Pics r not a match." The young lady was not Oksana. *Damn,* he thought, *I thought we had her*. The disguise had fooled CCTV.

Zoey's hands were shaking as she tried to concentrate on the road while constantly checking her side-view mirror. She called Myko to point out her turn one mile ahead. Convinced the girl was not Oksana, Oleg continued straight, following Mykola toward the airport. Zoey breathed a sigh of relief for herself, but now she worried about Mykola. She called him to let him know.

"I see him," Mykola said. "I think your new look worked. If he was a spy, he didn't recognize you."

"Now I'll worry about you! He's following you."

"He can't do anything to me, love. You're his target. When I get home, I'll start a rumor that I've found a new lover. If you hear the rumor, know it's just my way of protecting you until I can come to you."

"Please be careful, Myko!"

"And you, my love."

Although Marina's software did not identify the girl, Oleg wasn't ready to give up. As he sat on the plane to Cleveland, it occurred to him that Oksana could have had a makeover so complete it fooled their software. He kicked himself for being so easily fooled.

When his plane landed in Cleveland, he called Mischa. "I'm not 100 percent sure that the young woman I saw was not Oksana. I'm going to need you to go to Colorado and search the area where I last saw her. Can you leave tomorrow?"

"That's pushing it. I've got martial arts classes all week. And a blind search could keep me there for weeks. Or even months!"

Then Oleg called Demyan to tell him his suspicions. "Mischa has classes to teach. Any idea how I can get someone out to Colorado to search for her?" He proceeded to fill Demyan in on what he saw and where the girl turned east.

"We've got sleeper agents in Colorado. Much more practical than sending one of our agents on an uncertain mission on the other side of the country. A married couple lives in a suburb of Colorado Springs. I'll give the wife a timetable, so we don't just search indefinitely. I'll set it up for a month or two only. Remember, it could be a different girl entirely."

Oleg was relieved to have it off his shoulders and without even a reprimand for not nabbing the girl.

CHAPTER 36

MAY-AUGUST 2017

Alina Sokolova began her search for the girl in Lyons. If not for the road closure, Agent Sokolova would surely have started looking east and north of Estes Park. The indirect route her prey had taken at least bought Zoey some time.

Oleg remembered the first three letters on the license plate, though he had bumbled and forgotten the numbers. So, Alina searched for the license plate letters BRU on a silver Honda Fit. She hoped to find the girl and conduct surveillance before her window of time ended. Russians did not give up easily. Street by street, house by house, parking lots, and parking garages. When she felt she had exhausted her search in areas surrounding Lyons, she moved to towns farther south and east. Fortunately, Zoey had traveled north.

CIA agents had spotted Oleg while he was in Colorado and were keeping close tabs on him. They had intercepted his phone calls with Demyan and immediately contacted Agent Abbott to warn her. Alarmed, Agent Abbott called Zoey.

"Zoey, I've just learned some distressing news. I'll be at your house in 15 minutes."

"Yes, ma'am," Zoey said, startled by the urgency in her voice. Suppose she knew of Mykola's visit!

When Agent Abbott arrived, they sat side by side on the couch. "I've learned that a Russian operative is closing in on you. She's south of Longmont now, but we suspect it's only a matter of time before she turns north and makes her way to Fort Collins. You're in danger, Zoey, so I've scrawled a quick plan." The agent opened a spiral pad. "You'll need to get rid of your car. We'll get you into a new-to-you vehicle. We have reason to suspect that the Russian operatives might know what kind of car you drive."

Zoey knew that the man they saw in Estes Park had seen her car, but she hadn't revealed that to Agent Abbott. "How do you know they know my car?" she asked, feigning innocence.

"We don't know, but she was spotted cruising slowly through Longmont, looking at vehicles parked on both sides of the street. We believe she must know your car's make and license. We've learned that she has a Russian name and a link to an operative in Cleveland, Ohio. That's enough to put us on high alert. I'm going to take your car with me today, Zoey, and leave my car here overnight. I'll return with a different car for you by tomorrow afternoon. Are you OK to stay home on Sunday until I return?"

"Yes, I can stay home until then."

"Very well, Zoey. I'll leave you the keys to my car in case of an emergency. We have the make and plates on the rental car the agent is driving, so we'll be keeping our eyes on her. It would be a good idea for you to keep an eye out for her, too. She's driving a dark blue Toyota Corolla." She jotted the plate number for Zoey. "Be sure to let us know immediately if you should spot it. And get out of sight quickly in case she has a picture of you. I'm sorry about all this."

Zoey was certain that the operative did, in fact, have her picture, but she didn't reveal that to Agent Abbott. "Oh, Zoey, you've really messed up this time," she murmured to herself after Agent Abbott had left

On Sunday, a maroon Subaru Outback arrived at Zoey's house. Agent Abbott delivered the keys to her and said, "I'm afraid we've also decided we have to move you, at least temporarily, to an apartment in Cheyenne, Wyoming. The operative has begun moving her search northward."

"Wyoming? But I'm registered for evening classes at Colorado State at the end of August. Also, Croydon Prep starts up around the same time. I hope I can keep those obligations!"

"I know, Zoey. Hopefully we'll have an all clear by then. We'll be watching Agent Sokolova. We're hoping she gives up soon, but Cheyenne is less than an hour's drive. You may have to commute for a while. Do you think you can manage that?"

"Yes, I suppose that could work. When will I move?"

"Can you pack up your absolute essentials this evening? We'd like to have you out of here tomorrow morning."

"OK. I'll be ready," Zoey said reluctantly.

⅄

By 9:00 the next morning, Zoey was carrying her satchel and rolling a large suitcase into a small condo on West Prosser Road in Cheyenne, Wyoming. She had followed Agent Abbott, who came in to help her get settled. The condo was small but furnished, of course, and completely stocked with towels and linens. The kitchen had all the pots, dishes, and utensils Zoey could need.

After Agent Abbott helped Zoey unpack and get organized, she drove around Cheyenne to show her the downtown area a couple of miles away and the nearest shopping area. They stopped at L'Osteria Mondello at lunchtime for pizza.

"Well, do you think you can be happy enough here in Cheyenne for a while?"

"It's a little overwhelming, but I'm used to being lonely. I feel like we're in cowboy country, just like the old cowboy shows I remember seeing in Ukraine when I was a kid. I'll get an Internet connection so I can do some research and my homework, and maybe get in some sightseeing."

"Just no social media! And keep sightseeing to a minimum for now, I'd say. Keep your eyes open for the Toyota and for this woman." She handed Zoey the picture the CIA had provided her. "We'll be in touch, and of course, we'll let you know when it's safe to come home. This is one of our safe houses for temporary use. We keep our eye on it, so you'll be safe here, but call me if you see any suspicious activity. I think the operative will give up the search soon, after she realizes she can't find your car."

"I'm just glad you found out about her! I wonder if she would have found me if you hadn't let me know!"

"We'll try not to think about that, shall we?" Agent Abbot said, smiling at her. "Unfortunately, now that we know they are still actively searching for you, we'll be stepping up our surveillance."

"Oh, great. I already feel like a prisoner, watched from all sides."

After they each had a couple of pieces of pizza, Agent Abbott took her to the nearest Walmart to stock up on some groceries. She stopped at the hat department and bought Zoey two wide-brimmed sun hats. "Wear these with sunglasses when you are out and about," she said. Then she took Zoey back to the condo.

The moment she was alone, Zoey called Mykola.

"Zoey! Is something wrong?"

"Yes, in fact, everything is wrong. They've just moved me to a condo in Cheyenne."

"Cheyenne? Wyoming? Why?"

"They learned a Russian operative is searching for me. They traded in my car and got me another one."

"Do you know anything about the operative?"

"Just that it's a female named Alina Sokolova. I have the description of her vehicle and a picture of her, so I'll be on the alert. Apparently, she's searching for a Honda, so she won't recognize the Subaru I have now. But I know she has my updated picture. I didn't tell my advisor, but the woman is connected to the guy who followed us out of Estes Park. Oh, Myko," she lamented. "I guess we can't see each other anymore, at least for a very long time, possibly many more years. Maybe you need to move on with your life," Zoey said, getting choked up with so many conflicting emotions bombarding her at once.

"Don't say that Zoey! You're everything to me. We'll meet again before too long, I promise." It was a promise Mykola hoped he could keep.

When August arrived, Zoey commuted from Cheyenne to Croydon Prep and to Colorado State University for her evening education classes. The round-trip commute added two hours to her workday. By the time she piled class prep and studying on top of that, she had no time left to be lonely. She barely had time to eat and sleep.

Mr. Sobol had graduated and was now teaching at Colorado State, though he had applications at several larger schools in hopes of finding a tenure track position. Zoey saw him on campus occasionally when she walked to class. "How's your teaching going, Zoey?" he asked when they bumped into each other one evening.

"Very well, thank you. The students are enjoying some of the games you gave me to help them with the language. I learned lots from you. I think they like me OK."

"I'm sure they love you. You're so much nearer their age than I was."

It was true that Zoey was not that much older than her students and able to keep up with the latest trends. At least that part of her life couldn't have been better.

But she always had the feeling she was being watched when she was in Fort Collins. Agent Abbott called and told her one day, "Alina is retracing her steps, and checking CCTV cameras. Be sure to wear floppy hats and sunglasses wherever you go."

Zoey was getting more and more paranoid, hiding beneath hats and keeping her head down in stores and parking lots. Everyone began looking like Alina to her: short brown hair, bland expression, no distinguishing features she could make out.

The CIA learned that Alina was not acting alone. The SVR had assigned agents throughout northern Colorado.

"I'm sorry to say we have to change your looks again," Agent Abbott told Zoey a few days later. "They've increased the size of their team, so we've had to increase the size of our surveillance teams also. I'll pick you up Saturday morning at 8."

When she picked Zoey up to see their disguise artist on Saturday, she explained, "The stylist will redden your hair and change your contact lenses to green. He'll also add extensions to your hair, so you'll have long hair again, only auburn."

"I'm beginning to feel like a chameleon!" Zoey moaned.

The auburn dye on hair and eyebrows, followed by the tedious application of auburn extensions, took nearly the whole day. Then the makeup artist used a lighter foundation and taught Zoey how to dot freckles on her face with a special crayon. She was beginning to feel as if she were no longer even Zoey! Or Oksana! Or whoever she was!

One evening, as she was driving back to Cheyenne after class, Zoey spotted a dark blue Corolla. She quickly turned in at a ranch house and watched as the Corolla slowed down but drove on past the house. Zoey watched the car driving slowly on as she walked to the door and rapped. An older woman answered, and Zoey said, “Excuse me ma’am, but I think I’m lost. Can you tell me how far it is to Wellington?”

“Oh, honey, I’m afraid you passed that about 15 miles back.”

“Oh drat, how could I have missed it. I’m so sorry to have bothered you. Thank you so much for your help.”

“No problem, honey.”

The Corolla was out of sight, so Zoey backed out and turned south, back toward Fort Collins. She called Agent Abbott and told her she’d been followed.

“Have you lost her?”

“I believe so. She kept going slow when I stopped at a house and pretended I needed directions. After she was out of sight, I turned back and found an alternate route back to Fort Collins. I’m not sure if she drove past the house anymore or not. Now I’m afraid to go to Cheyenne. She could still be watching the house where I stopped.”

“Meet me at Avogadro’s at the corner of Mason and Corbin Alley. I can be there in 30 minutes.” When Agent Abbott got off the phone, she contacted the agent assigned to that area and told him to surveil houses 15 miles north of Wellington.

⅄

Over veggie subs and wine at Avogadro's in Fort Collins, Agent Abbott told Zoey they'd put her up in a motel for the night. "You can go to work from there tomorrow morning. I brought you a change of clothes in my car. You're about my size, I think."

"Have I told you defection sucks?"

"I know, sweetie. Just remind yourself of the alternative."

"Seriously. I don't know how much more of this I can take before I give up and go home."

"Don't say that, Zoey. Home won't be what you remember ever again."

Alina and others continued to comb the towns and the streets, looking for the silver Honda Fit. They spent the month of August and into September in Loveland, then on to Fort Collins. Alina called Oleg periodically to check in. Of course, now the CIA had tapped Alina's phone and knew that she was losing hope.

But Oleg was not giving up. He called Demyan to report on Alina's progress. "We'll have to assume Oksana got rid of her car. Or maybe she had a rental when I saw her. Marina is hacking CCTV in Fort Collins, so we can spot her in any store she goes into, or where she works, and even at all the ATMs in town. Tell the other agents to continue awhile longer, too."

CHAPTER 37

OCTOBER 2017

One evening, Mykola called Zoey's burner phone, all excited. "Listen to this, Zoey. We have a sliver of light! The UN and some other agencies have the location of the bomb, and they're working on negotiating a prisoner swap: Swapping the bomb and some pro-Russian separatist prisoners for Vlad and some resistance prisoners. Isn't that wonderful news? It could take a couple of months, so we'll have to be patient. The second Minsk Protocol failed, and talks in Belarus have broken down for now, but my handler thinks the bomb will sweeten the pot and bring Russia back to the table. I'm hoping Vlad is freed. Plus, if Russia gets the bomb back in its possession, maybe they'll give up looking for you! After all, your only mission was to help them find that bomb. I hope you can wait awhile longer! But be hypervigilant! I couldn't bear for them to find you now."

"I'll wait, Myko. As long as you still love me."

"You're my life and my hope, Zoey. I'll call you soon. Know that I'm with you and thinking of you always."

CHAPTER 38

OCTOBER 2017

Across the pond, Vlad was feeling more hopeless for the prisoners and for all of Ukraine. Every so often, Avel, one of the guards, would smuggle a newspaper to the prisoners. Avel had been a pro-Russian sympathizer, but as he watched atrocities continue and escalate, his loyalties began to vacillate. He dared not quit his job if he valued his life, but he let the prisoners know he was secretly on their side now.

Thanks to the *Den,* the Kyiv newspaper that Avel smuggled into the prison barracks, the prisoners had learned of another munitions depot explosion in September in Kalynivka, similar to the blast in Balakliya in March. The recent blast happened in the west-central portion of Ukraine, far from the Donbas and the east, where most of the separatist fighting was occurring. Did the broadening of scope mean the Russians were encroaching farther into Ukraine with hopes of annexing the whole country? A bad sign, atrocities happening so far west and far from the eastern Donbas region. Thirty thousand people had been evacuated this time, many injured, others lost or dead. Vlad regretted not being there to help. He feared the other munitions depots that he oversaw were likely in Russia's sights as well. He particularly worried about the depot where the nuke was hidden. An explosion at that depot could spread radiation over at least a ten-mile radius.

Reports in *Den* informed the prisoners that conflicts outside the prison had escalated by half in 2017 compared with 2016. The agreements at Minsk were forgotten as Russian weapons and rocket launch systems still poured into the country and put the civilian population as well as the resistance at risk. Civilian casualties grew as direct attacks targeted schools and hospitals. Food was scarce, especially in the occupied areas.

Vlad had been feeling hopeless and helpless until Mykola's letter about a prisoner swap arrived. He found Mykola's letter tucked into a rations box from Anya's organization. To think that there may be negotiations for a prisoner swap and that the bomb might seal the deal! That is if the Russians didn't blow it up first. He didn't wish for his freedom in order to escape danger; he wanted freedom so he could get back with his comrades in the resistance. He wanted to continue overseeing logistics and to keep the Russians from taking Ukraine, or any more parts of Ukraine, now that the Donetsk and Luhansk regions were already claimed by Russia. Vlad was concerned that the world didn't care, that no one outside Ukraine had any idea of the struggle they were engaged in.

With meager rations, all the prisoners had lost weight consistently over the months of their detainment. The injured were more at risk and slower to heal because of the deficiency of nutrients. Medical supplies were in short supply. Antibiotics nonexistent.

Every time a box of rations arrived from some generous organization or another, the men reveled in the crackers and cheese, the coffee and creamer. Sometimes they would find a canned ham. Often, they found beef jerky. Oranges and apples were passed around on the rare occasions they arrived.

That night after lights out, Vlad shared the news with his fellow prisoners in hushed tones: "America is attempting a prisoner swap for the bomb. Maybe we can leave this hell hole soon." Even the badly injured perked up at the news. Maybe there was hope for them yet. Bolstered by full stomachs from the box Anya had sent and the prospect of possible release, everyone slept well that night. The usual moans of men in misery were much diminished, at least for a night.

The next day, their lightened moods were shattered again. Separatist guards announced that today would be the day for some "questions," their euphemism for torture. Two or three at a time, the men were handcuffed and dragged off. Within the hour, they had each come back on stretchers and been dumped on their cots. Word was that the men were stripped naked, their ankles and wrists shackled to the wall. When the guards didn't like the answers they got, they beat the prisoners with batons.

That afternoon, when it was Vlad's turn, he experienced the torture firsthand. He was blindfolded and ordered to strip. After facing him against the wall, the guards pulled the straps tight enough around his wrists and ankles to cut off circulation. He had undergone interrogation before, but nothing this extreme.

"OK, Domitrovich, we know you have location of nuke, and you are going to tell us where is, da?" They must not have gotten the memo about the prisoner swap.

"They moved it after I was captured. They aren't stupid, you know."

Whap!—across his back with the baton. "We know this is lie. Every lie means one more whap, da? Where is bomb?"

"I don't know."

Whap.

This went on for thirty minutes until he was unshackled and fell to the floor in a heap. "We see you later, more cooperative, I advise. Dudnyk!" he called, and Leonid Dudnyk, the prisoner next to Vlad, turned to the wall for his turn.

The guards grabbed Vlad under each arm, hoisted him onto a stretcher, piled his clothes on top of him, and carried him back to his cot. The prisoners were beaten, removed, and returned to their cots continuously until 5 PM.

One of the prisoners asked the guard where he learned such torture. "From the Americans," the guard said with a sinister laugh. "OK, boys, we see you tomorrow, da?" Then, as quickly as they had arrived, the guards disappeared. Ten men lay groaning on their cots, while those left unscathed tended solemnly to the wounds of the tortured. Everyone knew their turn would come.

After the guards were gone, Avel, the sympathetic guard of their ward, carried a gallon of water into the ward, some antiseptic, and some rolls of gauze he had confiscated. He didn't dare stay to help, but the prisoners put the supplies to good use.

CHAPTER 39

OCTOBER 2017

Within a few days, some of Vlad's wounds became infected. With no available antibiotics, his fever continued to rise higher until he became delirious. Avel, who had been a nurse in Odesa before the unrest, was able to convince the guards to move him to the infirmary set up in a second-floor meeting room for the very ill.

Avel, who had befriended Vlad, decided to inform the International Red Cross covertly. "Please, we have a prisoner who is delirious from infections after being beaten. I'm afraid he won't survive without antibiotics."

The International Red Cross, having been granted the right by the third and fourth Geneva Conventions to visit prisoners of war, made an unannounced visit following Avel's call. Several men in the infirmary were badly in need of medical attention, but none in more dire need than Vlad. By the time the Red Cross arrived, his fever had risen to dangerously high levels and his blood pressure to dangerously low levels. He drifted in and out of consciousness, spouting hallucinatory pleas to get the bugs off him. Red Cross workers quickly attached an IV and administered blood tests, confirming their fear that he had septicemia. They knew he needed 24-hour care, which he clearly couldn't get here.

Dr. Patel told Avel, "Vladyslav Domitrovich must be moved to a hospital immediately or his organs will shut down. We must also take Andrii Petrenko, who lags behind Vladyslav in urgency by only a few days."

Avel volunteered to take Dr. Patel to the Commandant's office to convince him to release Vlad and Andrii. The other men who had been beaten were not as ill, having escaped severe infection, but the Red Cross supplied them with enough medical supplies, bandages, and antiseptics to change dressings regularly.

At first, the Commandant wouldn't budge. "Absolutely no one is to leave here. Nyet!"

"Excuse me, Sir," Dr. Patel said, "but according to the Geneva Convention, if either of these men dies against our advice, you could be charged with war crimes. We need to monitor Vladyslav Domitrovich 24 hours a day, put him on IV antibiotics, administer oxygen, possibly intubate him. Otherwise, his blood pressure will continue to drop, his organs will begin to fail, and he will die. The other case, Andrii Petrenko, is nearly as ill. He has the early stages of sepsis, and if you insist on keeping him here, he will also die. It is your guards who have put these men in this condition, and I must insist that you comply."

The Commandant weighed his options for a few moments. Finally, deciding he'd rather not be tried for war crimes and determining there were indeed no good options, he agreed to let them go. "Very well, doctor. You can take them to military hospital in Simferopol." Russians had seized that Crimean hospital in 2014.

"We'll helicopter them immediately."

"But I must send a guard with them. To keep an eye on them, da?"

Avel, standing beside Dr. Patel, said, "I'm a nurse. I will volunteer to guard the men, sir."

"Very well, Sergeant. You will accompany the prisoners. You will report to me daily. You will be held responsible for any infractions."

"Yes, sir," said Avel. "I'll ask Sergeant Stepan Bondar to take my shift, if that's OK, sir."

"Very well. Inform him of the change." The Commandant returned to the papers on his desk. "You're dismissed," he said.

When Avel introduced Dr. Patel to Sergeant Stepan Bondar, the doctor told him, "We'll check back with you in a week to make sure these other patients are recovering."

Avel took a few minutes to inform Stepan which injured prisoner needed what, while Dr. Patel and the Red Cross staff prepared the two patients for the journey. Avel had purposely chosen Stepan because they were friends, and Avel knew Stepan to be nearly as sympathetic to the prisoners as he was. He would take good care of them.

Vlad and Andrii were transported by gurney to the Red Cross helicopter. Avel sat between them on their flight. "We're going to get you help at the hospital, so you'll recover. You'll be fine," Avel told Vlad, who was drifting in and out of consciousness. Avel hoped he hadn't lied to him about recovering.

The helicopter arrived at the military hospital in Simferopol an hour later. Having called ahead, Dr. Patel found beds waiting for their patients, one in ICU for Vlad and another in a ward for Andrii. Avel stationed himself outside Andrii's room to maintain the appearance of a strict pro-Russian guard. Doctors immediately put an oxygen mask on Andrii and started his IV.

In ICU, critical care nurses sedated Vlad, and the doctor intubated him. Once he was stabilized and monitored, he could have visitors twice a day for ten minutes. Avel availed himself of those precious minutes to check on Vlad and was disturbed by the repetitive swiiiish, thump thump, swiiiish, thump thump of the ventilator. Vlad lay in an induced coma, his chest lurching mechanically up and down as air was forced into his lungs.

Watching Vlad struggling for his life, Avel became reflective. He had considered Vlad a friend, and yet they had been enemies in this war. He couldn't bear for his friend to die. He couldn't help seeing that the country he was fighting for would be responsible for Vlad's death and so many others. His loyalty had been slipping for some time, but now he wondered how he could go on. And yet to defect meant certain death. The lack of options left him deeply depressed. All he could do was go on as he had been, helping the prisoners as much as he could while feigning loyalty to the country he no longer respected.

CHAPTER 40

NOVEMBER 2017

Continuing to violate the Minsk ceasefire agreement, Russia and the separatists intensified their armed aggression in November, hitting the Donbas with grenade launchers, anti-tank missile systems, and barrel artillery, even hitting residential areas. Talks were stalled again. It looked as though the prisoner swap was off, for now anyway.

Mykola called Zoey after he read about the latest violation of the ceasefire. "Oh, Zoey, I'm broken-hearted. The fighting in eastern Ukraine has escalated. I'm afraid the prisoner swap was a false hope. Russia will never allow it now. They're so determined to annex Ukraine that they keep breaking the ceasefire."

"I know, Myko. I'm afraid it won't ever end."

"It can't go on forever. One day, it has to stop, one way or another. The question will be whether we even recognize our country after that. Or will it be a part of the Russian empire again? And poor Vlad. Will he ever get out of prison?"

Mykola wasn't aware that his friend lay in a Russian military hospital in Simferopol, Crimea, recovering now from septicemia. Fortunately, with hospital care, Vlad's condition was improving, and he had been moved from ICU into a room he shared with Andrii while Avel stood watch outside. Both patients were improving and would be returned to the prison soon. Avel filled them in on the ceasefire breach, the heightened warfare, and the postponed negotiations, so both men were in poor spirits. But both were alive. The separatists hadn't managed to kill them yet.

The future looked bleak for Mykola and Zoey as well. Zoey had been allowed to move back to Fort Collins, so she no longer had to make the long daily commute. Investigators were now following Alina's rental on GPS tracking devices, so they knew where she was at all times. Alina had passed back and forth in front of the house where Zoey had stopped one time, once pulling into the driveway and remaining for several minutes, possibly inquiring about the young woman who had stopped there, before she apparently gave up on that location and moved farther south, back to Loveland. But Zoey knew there was a surveillance network now made up of sleeper agents, so she never lost the feeling that she was trying to elude someone, and she didn't even know who.

"Myko, do you think I could rent a car, drive to the airport at night, and take an early morning flight to somewhere near you? I would leave my car at home in case they know what I'm driving now. Could we safely meet? Christmas break will be here in a month, and I can't imagine another Christmas alone and isolated."

"It's something to think about. Do you think you could escape surveillance?"

"I think I can avoid the Russians. Sometimes I think the CIA is just as much of an annoyance. It seems like they're watching my every move. I know they're protecting me, but they also imprison me."

"OK, Zoey. Let's think positive about a Christmas meeting. I think it's worth at least some risk just to maintain our sanity."

"Oh, Myko, the thought of a meeting will keep me going until then."

"Just don't get your hopes up too much. I couldn't bear to see you get hurt if it doesn't work out."

Meanwhile, things were still in flux in Ukraine. So angry was Putin about the U.S. and European sanctions placed on Russia after the annexation of Crimea that he was escalating attacks on Ukraine. He seemed to have no interest in negotiating a prisoner swap. Both Minsk agreements were repeatedly broken, and Germany and France, in trying to keep the terms of Minsk II, were no longer supplying arms to Ukraine. At the same time, Putin was planning to build a land bridge to Crimea. Russia had been trying to annex the port of Mariupol in Donetsk for several years. They occupied it briefly in 2014, but the Ukrainians retook it and have held the separatists off since then. Not only was Mariupol Ukraine's principal port on the Sea of Azov, but also it was the site of steel mills and agriculture essential to Ukraine's economy, so Ukraine must hold it, whatever the cost.

⅄

A week later, Anya called Mykola with exciting news. "Myko, our organization has learned that Putin has suddenly had a change of heart, called the Russian separatists, and ordered a prisoner swap after all.

"Hallelujah!" shouted Mykola. "I was losing hope that it would ever happen. What could have changed his mind so suddenly? I wonder if the lost bomb sweetened the pot."

"It may have," said Anya. "Word is that Putin is godfather to the daughter of the Ukrainian oligarch Medvedchuk, the Russian sympathizer who requested the swap. I don't know what his reason was for the request."

"Do you know where it will take place? And when?"

"Near Horlivka. Vlad's prison is not far from there. It may take some time to work out the particulars, so we have to remain hopeful. Since the order comes from Putin himself, I feel certain the swap will happen."

"This is the greatest news! I'm going to call my handler to see if the nuke is part of the deal."

They signed off, and Mykola dialed Agent Mitchell. "It's Mykola. I've had an exciting morning. I just learned that a prisoner swap is being negotiated near Horlivka. Do you know if the bomb is part of the deal?"

"Yes, a prisoner swap! Isn't that fantastic news, Mykola? I'll look into whether the bomb is part of the deal and get back to you ASAP."

Mykola then called Zoey again to bring her up to date. "Zoey, my love! I've just learned the most wonderful news!

Putin has ordered—ORDERED—a prisoner swap near Vlad's prison! Oh Zoey, it sounds too good to be true, but it is an ORDER! From PUTIN! How much more certain could it be than that?"

"Oh, Mykola! Such wonderful news! If they find their stupid bomb, maybe they'll be less interested in finding me! Oh, Myko! Could it be?"

"It must be. Putin's orders must be followed. My handler is looking into whether the order had anything to do with our nuke. He's going to call back. I'll let you know immediately."

"Yes, yes, Myko. The very moment you learn."

CHAPTER 41

DECEMBER 2017

December had arrived, the month everyone had set their hopes on. Vlad, to have the bomb returned and be released; Zoey, to possibly be less of a target; and Zoey and Mykola, to be together at last. No one had received word of how the swap was progressing—or even if it had been stalled again.

Finally, Agent Mitchell called Mykola to tell him that the bomb was indeed the catalyst for the negotiations. "The head of the Donetsk People's Republic announced in a summit in Moscow that an agreement has been reached. Ukraine will exchange 237 pro-Russian separatist prisoners and the bomb for 74 Ukrainian prisoners," he told Mykola.

"Sounds a little one-sided to me. Do you know when it will take place?"

"It's planned for the end of the month. We'll hope nothing changes before then."

"Yes, we'll hope the agreement holds. It's impossible to trust anything Putin says."

Mykola got off the phone and called Zoey. "It looks like the prisoner exchange will take place at the end of this month."

"Oh, Myko! Can it really be true? I'm afraid to hope."

"Don't ever give up hope."

"Do you think I can plan a trip over Christmas break?"

"Let's plan a tentative trip."

"Oh, Myko, I don't think I've ever been so excited. Maybe the end will come soon."

Zoey's days were bright and airy after the phone call. The hours seemed to fly by and feel endless at the same time. Three weeks to wait. She wanted to book her flight but was afraid her hopes could be dashed any day.

She called Agent Abbott to alert her that she would be going. "Don't try to stop me. I've made up my mind. It's urgent that I go." It was only a slight fib, she reasoned. It felt pretty urgent to her.

"I strongly discourage any visit to Ohio," Agent Abbott advised.

"I have to take the chance. The prisoner exchange at the end of the month will keep the Russians and the separatists occupied. Maybe they'll forget about me briefly. I'm not asking permission, just letting you know."

"Well, I don't advise it, but if you must, I guess you

must. Be sure to travel in the middle of the night. And be very observant for any faces that look familiar or that seem to be taking an interest in you. Wear a floppy hat. And remember, CCTV is everywhere."

"Of course."

"I can't forbid you to go, but please inform me the moment you're home safe. We don't want to blow your cover. And please give me your itinerary before you leave. I also need the number of your friend Mykola's burner phone, just in case something backfires. Again, I am not condoning this."

Zoey's students were getting restless and agitated. They were ready for Christmas break, too. Or maybe her own restlessness prompted theirs. Overall, their translations were a little sloppier, their homework showed less effort, and their test scores were lower. But everyone plodded onward.

"Try to hang in there a little longer, class," Zoey told them. "We're almost there."

"Yes, Ms. Parker," they groaned in unison.

Zoey thought she must be even more anxious than any of her students.

Mykola, too, was getting excited. He was eager to be rid of the bomb, eager to have Vlad released from the prison camp, and, most of all, eager to see Zoey, perhaps to be able to plan their future.

Meanwhile, the fighting in eastern Ukraine continued.

Ukraine had become a country divided, more akin to two distinct countries than one. Lviv, the capital of western Ukraine, was replete with Christmas preparations, as if the country, especially in the Donbas, weren't still torn by war. In Lviv, the JazzBez festival dominated the first week of December. As Ukrainians say, "Winter in Lviv starts with Jazz." The candle festival made a fairyland of the stunning medieval buildings twinkling with thousands of candles. Christmas parades filled the streets with colorful costumes, singing, dancing, and giant multicolored stars. The magnificent tree lighting festival at Sofiyvska Square belied the horror still taking place in the eastern part of the country.

On December 19, the night of the Christmas tree lighting in Lviv, heavy shelling was raining down on the Donbas region. Several civilians were killed, and houses were badly damaged, exposing survivors to freezing temperatures. Mykola read reports by the American special envoy to Ukraine that 2017 was the bloodiest year yet in the conflict and the most violent fighting since the Minsk ceasefire. How would they ever agree to the prisoner exchange?

In class discussions, Mykola's students became more attuned to the tragedies in Ukraine, tragedies about which most of the U.S. was virtually unaware. To lighten the mood, Mykola showed pictures of the Lviv Christmas parade. He brought poster board, wire, bright markers, and crepe paper streamers and let his class make their own Ukrainian Christmas stars based on resplendent images they found on the Internet.

The final papers he collected were surprisingly thoughtful and reflective, many contrasting the split country of

Ukraine and how it impacted their thinking about problems in their own country. But as he graded their papers, exceptional as they were, thoughts of Zoey kept distracting him. Whenever he became too rapt in reverie, he bundled up and took a long walk in the park, where he hoped to walk with Zoey again soon. Sometimes, he would take time to type a letter to send to Vlad through Anya's Care packages, though he never knew if Vlad received them and was still unaware of Vlad's recent serious illness.

Meanwhile, Zoey was grading final critical essays written in Russian about *The Death of Ivan Ilyich* by Tolstoy, the novella her classes had struggled through this semester. The translations were rough, so she had to make multiple markings on each page, though most students responded to Ilyich's final revelation that, rather than self-interest, compassion and empathy embody the authentic life. The task was tedious, but her thoughts, often sailing to Ohio and Myko's arms, kept her motivated to stick to it.

Both Mykola and Zoey peered up at the moon at the same time every evening to feel connected across the vast expanse between them.

CHAPTER 42

DECEMBER 2017

Vlad was still weak and suffering from PTSD after losing 14 kg, over 30 pounds, during his illness. He was hopeful he'd be part of the prisoner exchange but doubted he'd be able to continue the tasks he'd prided himself on before his capture. He would still need quite a long convalescence.

Avel, who had become a close friend, read to him and Andrii every evening and made sure they both choked down enough food to regain their strength. One night, when Vlad was restless and couldn't sleep, Avel fixed him some potato pancakes and hot herb tea in the kitchen, then sat by his cot to make sure he ate.

"Avel, I have nightmares about what will happen to us. I'm afraid I won't be able to help my comrades any longer. How can I? Barely 55 kg, 120 pounds, limping, and weak as a kitten."

"Maybe you can do something different for a little while to help them, Vlad. Office work maybe? Or comforting the convalescing? But don't worry, my friend. You'll get stronger and be as fit as ever before long. Here, another bite of deruni, please."

"You've been so good to me, Avel. You're good to all the prisoners. But we're supposed to be enemies."

"Let me fill you in on a little secret. You will keep it in confidence?"

"Of course, Avel."

"I am a Ukrainian pro-Russian separatist in name, but after watching the prisoners suffer at the hands of the separatists, seeing them broken up, recovering from lost arms, lost legs, seeing you near death, I no longer feel loyalty to a country so cruel as Russia. I'm hoping one day to seek asylum. If the separatists should learn of my defection, I will be tortured too, or even murdered. It's very important for you to stay silent about this."

"Of course! But what will you do?"

"I don't know yet, but I want to defect."

"Are you sincere? It could be extremely dangerous for you."

"I'm sincere, after many months of thought. After seeing you fighting for life on that ventilator, how could I condone such behavior by my comrades? You are more a friend to me than they ever were."

"If you're sincere, maybe that's what I can do if I get out of here. Maybe I can help you gain asylum in the U.S. Would you like that?"

"You would do that for me? I've always longed to see America. Maybe one day I could return home after the war ends."

"Don't lose hope, my friend. I'll think about this and see if I can come up with a plan. I have a good friend in the U.S. who might help us."

⅄

Meanwhile, in Russia, the SVR notified Andreii Andropov that they no longer needed to question the elusive Oksana Kovalska. The bomb was to be returned to Russia along with the prisoners, and Russia had spent enough time and money trying to locate Ms. Kovalska for interrogation.

On the other hand, they couldn't allow such an enemy of Russia to wander around freely in the U.S. The decision was made to continue to search for her. Once found, their instructions were simply to eliminate her.

In the U.S., three days before Christmas, Zoey drove a rental car to Denver airport under cover of darkness, keeping her eye on the rear-view mirror. She took a shuttle to her hotel, then flew to Cleveland Hopkins airport early the next morning, where Myko met her, this time with her long red hair and freckles.

"Who is this lovely creature?" he said, holding her at arms-length before pulling her to him in an embrace. "I love the flowing red hair! Every time I see you, you look entirely different."

"Oh, Myko. I'm still the same Zoey on the inside."

"That's good! Don't ever change on the inside. Does your handler know you've come?"

"She doesn't like it, but I told her I had to come."

An hour later, they were at Myko's apartment, where he fixed them a late lunch of lavash rolls: flatbread filled with chicken and cucumbers. They opened a bottle of white sparkling wine to celebrate the occasion, and he toasted the loveliest woman on the planet. He couldn't keep his eyes. . . or his hands. . . off her.

"Oh, Zoey," he kept saying. "We must be together soon."

"I hope so, Myko."

"If the prisoner swap and the long-awaited return of the bomb come off without a hitch, maybe they'll stop looking for you. We'll send up all our prayers over the Christmas season."

"This is the best Christmas ever! I finally have the Christmas spirit after years of despair. When are you planning to decorate the magnificent tree I saw in your living room?"

"I was waiting for you to get here. I thought we'd have some eggnog and decorate it tonight. Does that sound good to you?"

"Everything is so perfect. I love you so much, Myko." Zoey jumped up from her chair to go over and kiss him. He put a hand around her waist and drew her close.

"Ah, my love, I've waited for this moment," he said.

It had been such a long separation. They spent the afternoon catching up on each other's lives, their classes and students, their walks and favorite trails, their desires and hopes for the future, and of course, some passionate interludes sprinkled in. After a light dinner, Mykola fixed them eggnog, and they decorated the tree. All was gaiety and light-heartedness.

Finally, Myko turned to his concerns. "The fighting in

the Donbas has escalated, Zoey, so I'm still concerned about the exchange. I guess I can't believe anything anymore until I see it."

"Do you know if they're still negotiating?"

"I haven't read about negotiations breaking down, so I'm still hoping. I'm just getting impatient. It will happen someday, so I'm trying to keep the faith. We'll be together someday. Anyway, let's think positive for now and plan to go for a walk in the park tomorrow morning. Would you like that? I have extra hats, scarves, and sweaters if you think you'll need more layers."

"Yes, I would love that."

After a night of little sleep and more caressing, they ate a small breakfast of Kasha steamed cereal, then bundled up and trundled off to the park, where he showed her his favorite places along the path—the trails that led far up through the hills; the trail that curved off to the campus where he taught and that he walked to each day; the lake where he liked to sit on a bench and read student papers or a good book. Zoey remembered the area from her semester there but wanted to see every place he ever went to carry home in her memories in a few weeks.

"Remember Molson Hall, my office?"

"Of course, I remember it every day of my life. Please, let's go see it."

She was excited to see again his desk, the view from his window facing a grassy rise where students often strolled or sat in the grass to study. He showed her the safe where the phony coordinates had been stolen.

"I always imagine you here, sitting at your desk

grading papers, or talking to a student, or looking out your window at the grass and trees."

Later, they found a bench outside to sit and just enjoy each other's company, the campus, the fresh air, the occasional grad student passing by from the library.

"Have you heard anything from Vlad lately?" Zoey asked.

"No. I've smuggled several letters to him through Anya's organization, but of course, I haven't heard from him. He doesn't have any way to send a letter to me. I've also called his friend Dmytro, but he hasn't heard a word about Vlad, either."

"Next time you write, tell him I asked about him."

"Of course. He'll be glad to hear you're thinking of him."

Later that afternoon, Mykola got a call from his CIA contact informing him that the prisoner exchange was indeed going ahead as planned at the request of Medvedchuk, the Ukrainian with close ties to Putin.

"Oh, Myko. Maybe the day is coming when we can finally be together."

"Yes, my love. We'll keep praying."

The word was that Putin was also glad about the exchange since he expected his popularity to skyrocket before his election in a few months. He knew he would be reelected and could continue his plans to bring Ukraine back into the fold. He hoped to extend his reign for fifteen or twenty more years. Then he would have more power to have his way with Ukraine.

⅄

Anya invited Myko and Zoey to her home in Cleveland to celebrate Christmas Eve and stay overnight to celebrate the prisoner swap. She was having some colleagues over for eggnog, crudités, and sweet varenyky.

After hugs and greetings, Mykola said, "Tell me, Anya, have you heard anything about Vlad?"

"We don't hear much about the prisoners, but I did hear that Vlad is not well. He's had a bout with illness, but perhaps he's gaining strength."

"Do you know what kind of illness?"

"No, I didn't get any particulars. The man who delivered our recent package to them just sent word that Vlad is weak and has lost a great deal of weight."

"Oh, no. I hope he's OK. I hope he's part of the prisoner swap!"

"I'd think they would want to get rid of the sick ones. Less responsibility for them. We'll hope so anyway."

When the other guests arrived, the mood was unbridled gaiety, everyone chattering excitedly about the impending prisoner release. Guests brought their specialty, Ukrainian dishes, and more wine. Some of Anya's colleagues were also musicians and came with guitars, a keyboard, drums, and a violin. They supplied lively Ukrainian folk dances, some dancers wearing traditional embroidered costumes. The wine flowed freely, and every morsel of food was gone when the celebration finally ended in exhaustion at 3 AM. Some guests had already left. Others, having celebrated too much to drive, just slept on couches and chairs or on the floor.

Myko and Zoey collapsed into Anya's guest room bed in exhausted ecstasy, feeling more hopeful than they'd previously allowed themselves to feel. "Oh, my sweet Zoey. Rest well, my love." And they drifted into dreams of happier days.

After the lovers returned to Youngstown the day after Christmas, Myko received a text from Agent Mitchell: "The prisoner exchange is set for December 27. The Ukrainians will exchange the bomb and about 200 Russian separatist prisoners for 70 some Ukrainians. Your friend Vlad should be among them."

Mykola was joyful, even though he was appalled by the one-sidedness. What more could one expect from Putin? But still, Vlad free at last? Tomorrow? It was too wonderful. Maybe he would hear about it from Vlad's own lips soon.

The next day, the resistance and separatist fighters took a hiatus from shooting at each other to exchange prisoners. The suitcase bomb was successfully returned to Russia. The prisoners, Vlad among them, were free.

Vlad walked weakly toward the crowds until Dmytro spotted him and came pushing through the throng.

"Vlad? Is that you? You're so thin and pale."

"Yes, it's me. Let me hang onto your shoulder."

"Of course. Let's get you right to the car," Dmytro said

as he placed an arm around Vlad's waist to steady him.

"I have no place to go, Dmytro," Vlad said weakly.

"You will come to my place. My girlfriend is there, and she will help me nurse you back to health."

"Ha! Just like Dmytro! Amid all this fighting, he stills finds time for a girlfriend."

"One must keep one's sanity, yes?" Dmytro laughed.

"Good man. What is this wench's name, may I ask?"

"Her name is Sofia. The kindest woman I've ever met."

"Well, then, I must meet this Sofia."

CHAPTER 43

DECEMBER 2017

After the introductions and a brief chat about the ordeal that brought Vlad to them, Sofia excused herself and went to the kitchen to make tea and heat up some bigos stew for dinner.

"Do you still have my phone, Dmytro?" Vlad asked.

"Of course." He unplugged the phone on his desk and handed it to Vlad.

"I have to call Mykola and tell him I am free, free, free!"

"I know he'll be relieved. He's called every week or so to ask about you, but I've never had a report for him. I'll go help Sofia," Dmytro said, leaving Vlad to make his call.

Mykola saw the familiar number on his screen and assumed it was Dmytro. He was speechless when he heard Vlad's voice instead.

"Hello. Hello? Myko?"

"Vlad? Is this really you? My God, man, how the hell are you?"

"Yes, I'm a free man, though they still watch me. They

know the part I played in getting the bomb, and they know I oversaw munitions. I'm afraid I won't ever be able to return to my role before my capture. I probably won't even be able to return to my job. I've been very ill, Mykola, near death in fact."

"Near death!? My sister told me you were ill, but I was never able to get any details."

"Sepsis set in after the guards questioned me about my role in finding the bomb. I told them nothing, so they beat me and beat me some more. When the Red Cross came to inspect the prison, they insisted I go to hospital. They saved my life, but now I'm without hope. I want to go back to helping my comrades, but I'd be no use to them now. I'm very thin and weak now, Myko."

"I'm so sorry, Vlad. You shouldn't be going back to the militia, anyway, at least until you're really well!"

"I still want to help, Myko. I had a prison guard who became friends with the prisoners. He nursed me back to where I am now, sat with me nights, made sure I ate something. He was a pro-Russian separatist, but he's so disturbed by the cruelty he's witnessed of Russians and separatists toward the resistance that he wants to defect. I spoke to a man from the Red Cross when they returned to check on the sick prisoners. He told me to go to the U.S. Embassy in Kyiv if I want to help Avel gain asylum in the U.S."

"Yes, that's a wonderful idea. You must bring him here. At least let me nurse you back to health. It's not safe for you there now."

"Maybe it's best. He'll need friends to help him seek asylum. And I need a lot of convalescence. I can't help my comrades here, but maybe I can help Avel. If I were to be re-captured, I'd be a burden instead of an asset."

"That's exciting news, Vlad! I mean, not that you're ill, but that you're coming here to recover. You're both welcome to stay at my apartment."

"Do you have room?"

"I have an extra bedroom, and Anya has a cot I can borrow for your friend. What did you say his name was?"

"His name is Avel. He's been the best friend. He read to me every night while I was sick. He stayed with me and another badly wounded prisoner in the hospital. I know you'll like him. We'll be grateful for your help, Myko! But I'm told we'll need a sponsor to come to the U.S."

"Of course, I'll sponsor you and Avel! You're my best friend, for God's sake. I've been begging you to come here. And if Avel was so helpful, he's my friend now too! I'll be relieved to have you here and away from the fighting. You've been one of my constant worries.

"Oksana is visiting for Christmas break," Mykola continued. "She's standing right here asking to say hello. Her new name is Zoey."

"Hello, Vlad," she said when Mykola handed her the phone. "We're glad to hear you're coming here. We've been worried sick about you. Myko is ecstatic right now. Are you feeling better now?"

"Yes, it was an ordeal, though I'm much better. I'll be convalescing awhile yet, but I'm excited about coming to America! How are you? Zoey, is it?"

"Yes, I'm Zoey now. I'm well. Much happier now that I'm here with Myko for a short visit. Take care, Vlad, and come as soon as you can."

She handed the phone back to Mykola. "Listen, Vlad, maybe after you're here awhile, we can help bring your family here," Mykola said.

"Yes, I'd like that. OK, take good care, Myko, and maybe I'll see you soon!"

When they hung up, Vlad told Dmytro about his plans, then called Avel to tell him the good news. "Avel, we're going to the U.S. to stay with my best friend! He has invited us to stay with him and offered to be our sponsor. Get ready to pack your bags, my friend!"

"Can it be? You're such a good friend, Vlad. How can I ever repay you?"

"It's you I must repay. I owe you my life, Avel. Literally!"

Vlad began the process by making an appointment at the U.S. Embassy in Kyiv for the following Monday. In hopes Avel could find asylum at the embassy, Vlad told him to pack a duffle bag. That Monday, Dmytro drove the pair to Kyiv for their appointment.

"A gray car has been a couple of lengths behind us the whole way," Dmytro said as they neared the embassy.

"Fuck," said Avel. "They're after me. They want to find where I'm staying because poison or nerve gas draws less attention than bullets."

When they entered the embassy, Vlad said, "I have an appointment to talk to Agent Charles Nichols."

After a long introductory interview in a small office, Vlad and Avel were ushered into a large, well-appointed office. Still quite weak, Vlad leaned on Avel to walk.

"How may I help you, gentlemen?" Agent Nichols asked once they were seated.

"We've come to seek asylum in the United States," Vlad said, and then began his long story. "I'm Vladyslav Domitrovich and this is Avel Kushnir.

Vlad explained how he was injured by shrapnel, beaten, and nearly died as a prisoner of war during the resistance; how he helped to discover the nuclear bomb that had now been returned to Russia; and how well he was cared for by the former Ukrainian separatist guard, Avel, who was defecting.

Avel explained how the pain, suffering, and mistreatment of fellow Ukrainian prisoners, wounded or otherwise, had convinced him that he could no longer serve the interests of the pro-Russian separatists. He was now in agreement with the resistance and wanted to help Ukraine escape Russian annexation.

"The separatists have learned that Avel helped me and the other wounded prisoners," Vlad said. "It was easy for them to deduce that he had defected. In fact, we believe they followed us here today."

"Yes," Avel added, "I had to leave my job and hide out because the separatists plan to kill me as a traitor."

By this time, Vlad was near tears, so weakened were he and his defenses. "And now, I too am being surveilled by separatists," he said. "Can you help us, Sir?"

"We may be able to help you, but you'll have to find a sponsor in the U.S. Do you know anyone there?"

"My best friend is there, and he has agreed to sponsor us."

"That's a good start. He needs to file a petition for both of you with Immigration Services, and we'll go from there. Fortunately for you, Ukrainians are finding it easier to emigrate to the U.S. than most other nationalities because of the current animosity between Russia and the U.S.

"After USCIS approves the sponsor petition, follow the steps on this Immigration Visa Process link," Agent Nichols continued, handing Vlad the list with links and steps to take. "Send this link to your friend in the U.S. also." He circled the main link in red. "Many hoops to jump through, I'm afraid. It could take several months."

"But I'm in imminent danger of being killed right now as a traitor to the cause by the separatists," said Avel. "We were followed here today! Isn't there anything I can do to protect my safety until I can get a visa?"

"I'm also in danger," added Vlad. "I'm getting death threats since they learned I found and hid the bomb."

"There are a couple of possible paths," said Agent Nichols. "We can contact DHS for refugee admission. If that fails, we can request a humanitarian parole. These are temporary measures until you can get your visas. I'll begin that process. Until that time, we can only offer you temporary refuge at the embassy, just until you are out of imminent danger of death. Hopefully, by that time, either of the two temporary measures will be accepted."

CHAPTER 44

DECEMBER 2017

Vlad texted Mykola:

Myko, follow this link to begin sponsor procedure.

Thx, Vlad. He typed the link.

Mykola clicked the link and quickly skimmed the steps he'd have to take. Then he and Zoey worked together and completed all the steps. In a celebratory mood, the two of them walked down to Avalon Downtown, Mykola's favorite pizza and wine restaurant near campus, and a student hangout. It was early for supper, so the place was empty, awaiting the onslaught of college students who usually began arriving around 6:00 to liven up the joint. Mykola and Zoey chose a booth near the back and ordered an Italian Brier Hill pizza and a carafe of Riesling to celebrate their love and getting Vlad to the U.S.

"Oh, and I'll have a glass of water, please," Zoey called after the waitress.

"Certainly, ma'am."

"So, Zoey, I guess we can't make plans for me to move

to Colorado just yet. I know how frustrated you're getting. I wonder how long Russia will continue to look for a young Ukrainian woman. After all, you're not even Russian."

"Yes, but I was working for the Russian government specifically to get the bomb coordinates by tempting you. Unfortunately, you tempted me instead."

"But now they have the bomb. And they have Crimea. And it looks like they could soon have Ukraine, or at least the eastern parts of it. What more could they want from you? They got everything they wanted."

"Everything except my loyalty. And now they want my blood. I can never contact my parents again or they'll find me. I can never go home, or they'll kill me. They could even kill or torture my family, and I wouldn't know it."

"Oh Zoey, what have I done? My obsession with that bomb has destroyed your life and Vlad's life. And both your families' lives as well."

"On the other hand, we would never have met if you hadn't located that bomb," Zoey said, taking his hand. "But lots of unexplained deaths have happened to Russian defectors in other nations. We know Russia can reach anywhere. Anyone who has access to information that Putin wants to cover up is at risk anywhere in the world. His long arms reach far and wide."

"I'm so sorry, Zoey. But for now, let's forget Russia," Mykola said, hoping to lighten the gloom for now. "Let's make our last night together, for who knows how long, a night to remember fondly. Let's try to think positive, even though it's a struggle."

"Yes, all I can do now is think positive. Let's eat, drink, and be merry, as it says somewhere in the Bible," she said, snuggling up next to him.

"Sounds like perfect advice to me," Mykola agreed as they toasted. "Let's talk of love instead. Because I find I love you more every day."

Then Mykola put his arm around her and pulled her closer. She put her head on his shoulder. Mykola continued, "I will move to Fort Collins as soon as I feel it's safe, and we'll get married. Would you like that?"

Zoey didn't respond. Mykola thought it odd that she could have fallen asleep while he was proposing, so he gave her a nudge to wake her. That's when he realized she was limp in his arms.

"Zoey! Zoey!" he called, shaking her. She was unconscious. "Call 911," he hollered to anyone in earshot.

The ambulance arrived in ten minutes, which felt like two hours to Mykola. They were only a mile from the hospital, so the emergency crew began working on her in record time. Mykola told them he expected foul play since she was a defector from Ukraine. The ICU doctor was a Ukrainian immigrant who kept up with Russia's shenanigans in the news, so he ordered a blood test STAT, which confirmed his suspicion that she had been poisoned by a nerve agent, probably Novichok. He administered atropine and pralidoxime chloride to stop the action of the nerve agent, but he knew that wasn't a cure. After they hooked her up to various massive noisy machines to keep her alive, and he felt she was stable for the time being, he stepped out to the waiting room to inform Mykola of the diagnosis.

"My name is Dr. Koval. Your friend has been attacked by a nerve agent. We're doing everything in our power to save her. Police have been called in to protect against any further attack in ICU. She is heavily sedated to protect her from brain damage and so that her body can tolerate the heavy medical equipment we had to attach to keep her organs alive. She's intubated, of course. I'm afraid her prognosis is not good. It will depend on the next 48 to 72 hours. That and the young woman's constitution."

Mykola was devastated. She was told not to make the trip, but he had let her come. No, he had selfishly encouraged her to come. Once she was out of the watchful eye of the CIA, she was fair game. Oh, he never should have taken her out in public. But how could they have poisoned her? They must have followed her and Mykola to the restaurant. Could they have put it in the pizza? Or the wine? But he had no symptoms. She had asked for a glass of water but only took a sip or two. That must have been it. Thank goodness she didn't drink the whole glass.

Mykola called the restaurant to warn them. He advised them to throw away the glass she drank from if they had not already reused it. His heart raced as he worried about a more widespread poisoning. He spoke to the nurse at the desk to tell her he thought it was just a sip or two of water that caused the illness. "Please inform her doctor. Maybe since she drank so little, she might recover."

"I'll be sure he knows," she said.

He prayed. He called Anya. He called Vlad. Everyone he knew. They all promised to pray for her recovery.

All he could do now was return home and come back tomorrow morning for the ten-minute visit she was allowed to have at 10:00 AM and another at 2:00.

⅄

Back in his apartment, he could only sit and stare. He couldn't think. His brain seemed to shut down. He had never experienced grief, but this was surely grief. "She must live, she must live, she must live!" he moaned.

He suddenly jumped up and started ripping the decorations off the tree they had decorated, tears streaming down his cheeks. He pulled down the little angel that he had lifted Oksana to place on top. He tore off the lights and the tinsel, sobbing now as he threw everything haphazardly into the storage box. He was lashing out at reality, a reality he couldn't accept, couldn't change. Nothing, nothing could relieve the ache in his heart. How could he go on? He flopped face down on the bed and sobbed, "My God, My God!" What horror had he wrought?

CHAPTER 45

A week had passed, somehow, as they do, even to those who are grieving. Mykola visited the comatose Oksana twice a day for the ten-minute visit allowed in ICU. "No change," the doctor said. "We're doing everything we can." The days were interminable, each one a long struggle to get through. Soon he'd be back in school, and how could he possibly handle the classes, the faculty meetings, the lesson plans, the students?

In Cleveland, Demyan Ivanov, Oksana's handler in the U.S., was on his secure phone, praising Oleg Vasiliev for so admirably completing his mission. Oleg had never given up on the possibility that the young lady with short dark hair was Oksana after cosmetic surgery, despite Marina's determination that it was not her. Oleg had continued to surveille Mykola and had followed him to the airport, where he met the beautiful young lady with flowing red hair who visited for Christmas. Oleg was able to snap a picture, despite the floppy hat and sunglasses, and promptly forwarded it to Marina, who confirmed that this was indeed the same girl as the one with the dark pixie haircut.

He had reported his suspicions back to Demyan, forwarding him the pictures of the blonde Oksana, the dark-haired girl, and the redhead. Demyan was convinced enough to order the elimination of the lovely traitor. "You will receive a small vial of Novichok. You are well aware of the precautions you must take, da?"

"Da, I am aware."

"Very well. I trust you will follow this young couple wherever they go until you find a way to carefully add a few drops to her water or tea. How you will accomplish this is up to you but be sure that you don't touch the contents of the vial. If you exhibit the greatest professionalism and complete your mission, you will have a nice promotion. If you fail, of course, there will be penalties."

"I understand."

The next day, while Oleg had been watching Mykola's apartment, a stranger passed him casually, tipping his hat as he handed him a small paper bag containing the vial. Now he would have his chance.

Early that evening, the couple walked from Mykola's apartment to the pizza restaurant. Oleg stayed a good distance behind them since he knew he'd been spotted in Estes Park. He wore exercise clothes and a ball cap, so that if he were spotted, they might take him for a jogger or walker.

Inside the restaurant, the pair headed toward a back booth. Oleg took a seat at the bar in front, next to the waitress station. He purposely peered out the front window but could hear the couple chattering in the back. He also heard the young lady loudly add a glass of water to the order. This was his chance!

The waitress placed the water on a tray, along with place settings, then turned back to pour the carafe of wine. Oleg easily dropped a few drops from the vial into the glass undetected.

As a few students began wandering in, Oleg slipped out, his mission complete. He jogged happily back to his motel room and called Demyan.

"I have fulfilled my assignment."

"Well done. I'll be eagerly awaiting the outcome. For now, get back to Cleveland."

"Yes, Sir."

A week later, Oksana was still in a medically induced coma. Some of the best experts in nerve agent poisoning from around the world were advising on the case. Some of her readings were improving, but she was not out of the woods. Mykola continued visiting her during the two daily visiting times, talking to her about their future together. He had read that people in a coma could hear what was being said to them, so he came with plenty to talk about. He told her how things were going with Vlad and how he couldn't wait for her to see Vlad when he got to the U.S. He told her that USCIS had approved him as a sponsor for Vlad and Avel, and that the DHS had approved their refugee asylum in the U.S. They had passed their medical exams and succeeded in their interviews. He hoped she heard him, but of course, he had no way of knowing.

⅄

That evening, Vlad called Mykola. "Myko, we've jumped through all the hoops, and we are coming to the U.S.! Thank you, my friend, for helping us. We're in Poland now, and safely out of the hands of the separatists or the Russians."

"I can't wait to see you. Youngstown State is eager to interview you for a position in the sociology department! I've talked to Human Resources at Mercy Hospital, where Zoey is. They're interested in seeing Avel. It seems there's a shortage of nurses here."

"That's great news, Myko! But how is Zoey? Has she regained consciousness?"

"Oh, Vlad, they're keeping her in a medically induced coma for now. She's improving slightly, but if she survives, I'm afraid there could be brain damage. But she'll get better. I'm determined she will."

"I'm sorry to hear that, but I'm glad you're keeping a positive attitude. Avel and I have both been praying for her."

"Thank you, Vlad. I'll tell her when she wakes up." Mykola couldn't bear to say *if* she wakes up. She had to wake up.

"Maybe we should make other arrangements to stay? When Zoey comes back to your apartment, you won't want us hanging around."

"Oh, I don't know. I'll probably need the moral support. And maybe some other help. Let's leave it like it is for now."

"Well, hopefully we can go right to work and get our own places soon. But we'll help you in any way we can.

You're so kind to let us stay with you."

"It's my pleasure to have you here, and out of the hands of the separatists. Plus, I need company right now to restore my sanity."

"You've been a tremendous help! How can I ever thank you?"

"Coming here safely is all the thanks I want. I look forward to seeing you soon. And keep Zoey in your prayers."

"Will do, my friend."

CHAPTER 46

Agent Michelle Abbott was becoming frantic since Zoey did not return when she was expected. She called Mykola, using the burner phone number Zoey had left with her. Mykola had to break the sad news.

"My God!" cried Agent Abbott. "I'll be there as soon as I can. Where is she?"

Myko gave her the name of the hospital.

"I'll be in touch," she said before she hung up.

Two days later, when he went to visiting hours at 10 AM, he was told that Zoey was no longer there.

"She's gone!? How is that possible?"

"She was removed to an undisclosed location. We weren't given any reason or details."

"Why did you let her go?"

"You'd have to talk to the hospital administrator." She directed him to the administrator's office.

When someone led him into the office of the administrator, Mykola demanded to know what happened to Ms. Zoey Parker.

"Please calm down, Sir. Your name is?"

"My name is Mykola Kravchenkos. Zoey and I are engaged," he fibbed only slightly.

"Mr. Kravchenkos, Ms. Parker has been moved to an undisclosed location by order of the U.S. government. She is apparently in a government protection program. We are not able to divulge the location to anyone."

"Can you tell me how she is? Is she improving?"

"She has improved slightly but is still in a medically induced coma."

Mykola was beside himself. He couldn't see her anymore? He couldn't continue his long talks with her and tell her his plans for them when she recovered?

That evening, Agent Abbott called him on his burner phone. "I'm extending you the courtesy of a phone call because I know she thought a great deal of you, and you of her."

"Where is she? I need to see her!"

"We cannot risk disclosing her location, for obvious reasons. Our assignment is only to keep her safe. I'm sorry you won't be able to see her, but rest assured, she is receiving the absolute best care possible. I will call occasionally to update you on her condition."

"I've been talking to her every day," Mykola said. "I've heard that people in a coma can hear you when you talk to them. Can someone talk to her? Tell her that I am waiting for her to recover?"

"I'll see what I can do. I'm so sorry this happened, but she was warned not to make this trip."

"I know. And I encouraged her. Don't you think I'm kicking myself every day?"

"I also called to let you know we are placing a phony obituary in the local paper for Oksana Kovalska. Just remember, the woman you love is not Oksana Kovalska. She is Zoey Parker, and I feel certain Zoey Parker will recover."

"Thank you for warning me. I won't even look at the obituaries. I couldn't bear to. But if it keeps her safe, I'm all for it."

"Hopefully, the people looking for her will see it. I must go now, but I'll be in touch." And then the agent was gone.

Spring semester began, and Mykola somehow managed to keep trudging through the days. Agent Abbott called one afternoon to tell him things were looking more positive for Zoey's recovery, though she would need a great deal of care. "She will probably be disoriented, lethargic, possibly have some brain damage, and certainly some memory loss. All or most of the symptoms should improve over time with physical and occupational therapy. She could be in rehab for quite some time, though."

"I'll be waiting, however long it takes. But I'd like to marry her and take her out of the U.S., possibly to Canada."

"That could be a wise choice. The Russians believe she is dead, but there is still CCTV everywhere. Our counterpart in Canada is the Canadian Security Intelligence

Service, the CSIS. We coordinate fully with them. I can help arrange a transfer when she is well enough, if that's what you two decide."

"Whew. I like you better already," Mykola said.

"I'll be in touch," and she was gone again.

Mykola thought about Vlad's immigration process and began researching immigration processes for his class discussion the next day. He stopped what he was working on to also investigate emigration and political asylum in Canada. Could that be the light at the end of the long tunnel?

He learned in researching Canada's policies that Zoey would be eligible for political asylum since she was in danger in the U.S., and she would be protected by the CSIS. Mykola wasn't in imminent danger himself since he'd been a U.S. citizen for many years, but he could prove he was under surveillance and needed protection. Also, he had the education to be an asset to Canada in one of their universities, so if he and Zoey were married, he could enter Canada also.

He barely slept that night, his mind churning: Canada, Zoey, Vlad, Avel. It was becoming too much. Could any of it ever happen?

CHAPTER 47

A YEAR LATER

2019

The year 2018 had been a hard year for Mykola. And for Zoey. Zoey had indeed survived, but she had to retrain her brain to walk, to use her hands, and even to talk. She had no memory of being ill or even of the fateful day they ate pizza together. She had remained in rehab for most of the year, and finally, after being reunited with Mykola, the lovers were moved to a temporary safe house under CIA surveillance.

2018 was also a hard year for Russia. Russian citizens had grown increasingly dissatisfied with their government, leading to protests all summer for fair elections. A nuclear accident was covered up with secrecy and lies, much as the Chernobyl disaster near Pripyat, Ukraine, in 1986 had been. Forest fires raged through Siberia, and Arctic ice and permafrost melted in the record high temperatures.

Ukraine also had its problems. Pro-Russian separatists

still fought in the East with help from the Russians. But a charismatic 41-year-old named Volodymyr Zelenskyy won the election by a landslide, at least partially on his promise to restart peace talks with the separatists and to finally unite Ukraine. Some feared he would not be able to stand up to Putin during this chaotic time, with fighting still raging and Crimea already taken by Russia. An American president, fearing losing his upcoming election, offered Zelenskyy the weapons Ukraine wanted only if he would find dirt on the new, favored, American presidential candidate and his family. Zelenskyy refused. And so, those much-needed weapons were not forthcoming.

At the same time, Russia believed they had killed the spy they had assigned to learn the coordinates of the bomb that had long since been found and returned to Russia, but they had plenty of other political enemies to poison and imprison. As far as Russia's designs on Ukraine, however, they remained unchanged–Eastern Ukraine, the Donbas, was appealing to them. They also had the desire for a land bridge to cut off Ukraine's access to the Black Sea, essentially land-locking the country. Peace is a fragile thing, and Putin is a rapacious leader who still believes Kyiv is the true birthplace of Russia.

But Zoey and Mykola were safe, living in a safe house now, on the other side of Ohio in Springfield. Zoey was regaining her balance and her memory more rapidly now. Vlad and Avel were safely in Youngstown, having taken over Mykola's lease until they found places of their own. Both were gainfully employed in the jobs Mykola had found for them.

Several months later, when Zoey felt she was fully recovered, Mykola and Zoey made plans for a small wedding. They would marry in the chapel of the Greek Orthodox Assumption of the Blessed Virgin Church, which had recently decided to recognize the autocephalous Orthodox Church of Ukraine.

Vlad and Avel managed to get a short leave of absence from their jobs to travel to Springfield for the wedding, where Vlad would be the Best Man and Avel and Mykola's cousin Denys would be the Groomsmen. Anya was to be Maid of Honor, and Agent Michelle Abbott and the Balanchuks' daughter Galyna agreed to be bridesmaids. The Balanchuks, the dear friends of the Kravchenkos who had originally helped bring the family to the U.S., and Mykola's parents all came for the occasion, of course. Vlad's family had not immigrated to the U.S. yet, and sadly, Zoey's parents weren't there for obvious reasons. Zoey hoped to have them visit after she and Myko had safely moved to Banff, Alberta. She had not spoken to them since she left Ukraine.

Zoey and Mykola had their visas and had secured refugee asylum in Canada, thanks to some strings pulled by Agent Abbott. Zoey hoped to find a job teaching in Banff, if not in a high school, then teaching ice skating students. Mykola had already flown to Banff and secured an assistant professorship at Bow Valley College. For the first time since they'd met five years ago, Mykola and Zoey weren't constantly looking over their shoulder. Agents Abbott and Mitchell had secured protected status for the young couple in Canada, so they would have continued protection under the CSIS. The future for them looked bright indeed, but the same could not be said for their home country.

Zoey decided to wait until they were safely settled in Banff before calling her parents. The less they knew about her ordeal, the better. She decided never to tell them she had failed at her mission and defected. She would simply tell them she fell in love in the U.S. She knew they would approve of Mykola.

Mykola's father said he was ready to retire from PPG and might surprise them one day by showing up in Banff. Even Anya, whose job in Cleveland was less urgent for the time being, promised to visit them in Banff after they were settled.

And then it was official. Zoey and Mykola Kravchenkos were one, and Zoey proudly wore an official Ukrainian name again, Kravchenka.

After a flutter of toasts to the couple's health and happiness at the reception, the wedding party scattered to their various destinations for the night. Myko and Zoey headed to their honeymoon suite at the Marriott, where we shall leave them alone in their peaceful wedded bliss at long last.

AFTERWORD

Of course, unrest in Ukraine continued long past the wedding day of Zoey and Mykola. After Putin's reelection in 2018, amendments were ratified to keep him in power until 2036. With his newly granted power, aggression continued, with Ukraine in Putin's crosshairs, finally escalating to a buildup of Russian troops along the eastern border of Ukraine, throughout the annexed Crimea, in the Black Sea around Odesa, in the Sea of Azov around Mariupol, and in Belarus, Russia's ally on the north. Putin's apparent plan is to topple Zelenskyy and reinstall his ally, the failed Victor Yanukovych, to lead Ukraine once again.

Vlad and Mykola continued their correspondence about the increasing threat to their home country. They discussed Putin's embrace of Ivan Ilyin's mythology that a Russian takeover of Ukraine would be righteous: a good versus evil return to ancient Rus from a thousand years past. Putin rationalized that the West had broken laws, so laws had no meaning.

The future of Ukraine's country looks grim. Russian tanks and 190,000 troops attacked from the East, North, and South. Putin couldn't tolerate the election of the young Zelenskyy, who was determined that Ukraine become a peaceful democracy and hopefully a member of the EU. Following false Russian intelligence by Putin's top advisors, meant more to please Putin than to be accurate, Putin predicted the Ukrainians would accept the Russians as liberators and willingly surrender. How wrong he was.

Despite their happiness in their new lives, Vlad, Mykola, and Oksana grieved for their friends and families who remained in a war-torn Ukraine. Vlad was relieved when he learned his family had made the long, dangerous journey to Lviv and from there to Poland, where now they were working on emigrating to the U.S. to reunite with Vlad.

Today Ukraine is virtually being destroyed. Several million Ukrainians have fled to Poland, Hungary, and beyond, yet peace is not in sight. How many thousands have been killed or remain to be killed on both sides of the war? How many placed in "Filtration Camps," akin to Nazi Germany's Concentration Camps for Jews in WWII? And for what purpose?

Though the people inhabiting our story have a happy ending, their home country and the world have an uncertain future at best. Some have suggested that after Ukraine, Putin will attack other former Soviet states in hopes of reconstituting the Soviet Union. If this is the case, some predict we could be facing WWIII if it has not already begun.

The Russians are not winning. President Zelenskyy has determined that Russia will never take Ukraine. Ukrainians are giving their last ounce of courage and resolve to save their country. Russians may flatten the country, but they will never win the hearts and souls of the Ukrainian people.

Now the debate begins. Should the U.S. and our allies supply the Ukrainians with more weapons? Or should we, as Emmanuel Macron suggests, work toward "an exit ramp through diplomatic means?"

Slava Ukraini!

ACKNOWLEDGMENTS

Having done a great deal of research for this novel, it would be impossible to acknowledge every source that helped me. Much of my background came from news sources such as *The New York Times, The Washington Post, The Guardian, Reuters, CNN, NBC, MSNBC, PBS, BBC News, Kyiv Post, The Jamestown Foundation,* and *The Wilson Center.*

Timothy Snyder's books, *On Tyranny* and *The Road to Unfreedom*, were invaluable sources on Putin's philosophy regarding Ukraine.

Volodymyr Zelenskyy's election and determination, bringing hope for Ukrainian unity, was my inspiration in our world of turmoil.

I'd also like to acknowledge my husband, Joe, who helped form the idea for the story and helped me with getting started, researching, critical reading, advising, and moral support.

SOURCES CONSULTED

Abou-Sabe, Kenzi, Tom Winter, and Max Tucker. "What Did ex-Trump Aide Paul Manafort Really Do in Ukraine." *NBC News*, June 27, 2017.

Ball, Joshua. "Russia's Justification for the Annexation of Crimea." Global Security Review. GlobalSecurityReview.com, June 10, 2019.

BBC. "Ukraine's Ousted President Victor Yanukovych." bbc.com, Feb. 28, 2014.

BBC. "Navalny 'poisoned': What are Novichok agents and what do they do?" bbc.com, Sept. 2, 2020.

Budjeryn, Mariana. "The Breach: Ukraine's Territorial Integrity and the Budapest Memorandum." *The Wilson Center* wilsoncenter.org, Issue Brief #3.

Bagchi, Rounak. "Victor Yanukovych: Ukraine's Ousted President Who May be Russia's Pick After War." Indianexpress.com, March 4, 2022.

CNN. "Read Trump's Phone Conversation with Volodymyr Zelenskyy." cnn.com, Sept. 26, 2019.

Foer, Franklin. "Paul Manafort: American Hustler." *The Atlantic* theatlantic.com, Jan. 26, 2018.

Korniienko, Artur, and Jack Laurenson. "2014: Victorious Revolution Triggers Russia's War." *Kyiv Post kyivpost.com, Dec. 20, 2019.*

Olympics.com. "Oksana Baiul."

PBS. "A Historical Timeline of Post-Independence Ukraine." pbs.org, Feb 22, 2022.

Peace Corps. "Cactus Program in Ternopil, Ukraine. peacecorps.gov, Aug.7, 2019

Reuters. "Russia Must Not be Humiliated Despite Putin's 'Historic' Mistake, Macron says." reuters.com, June 4, 2022.

--- "Ukraine's Turbulent History Since Independence in 1991." reuters.com, Feb 24, 2022.

Smith, Alexander, and Yuliya Talmazan. "Where Will Putin Stop?" *NBC News*. nbcnews.com, Nov.29, 2018.

Socor, Vladimir. "Russia Smashing Ukraine into Pax Russia." *Eurasia Daily Monitor 19.39,* in *The Jamestown Foundation.* Jamestown.org, March 22, 2022.

Snyder, Timothy. *On Tyranny: Twenty Lessons from the Twentieth Century.* Crown Publishers, Feb. 28, 2017.

The Road to Unfreedom. Tim Duggan Books, New York, 2018.

United Nations Treaty Collection, treaties.un.org.

U.S. Citizen and Immigration Services. "Uniting for Ukraine." Uscis.gov

U.S. Department of Justice. "EOIR Review Electronic Access and Filing." justice.gov

U.S. Department of State: Department of Conflict and Stabilization Operations. "A Pathway to Defections." state.gov.

U.S. Institute of Peace. "Peace Processes." usip.org

ABOUT
ATMOSPHERE PRESS

Atmosphere Press is an independent, full-service publisher for excellent books in all genres and for all audiences. Learn more about what we do at atmospherepress.com.

We encourage you to check out some of Atmosphere's latest releases, which are available at Amazon.com and via order from your local bookstore:

Dancing with David, a novel by Siegfried Johnson

The Friendship Quilts, a novel by June Calender

My Significant Nobody, a novel by Stevie D. Parker

Nine Days, a novel by Judy Lannon

Shining New Testament: The Cloning of Jay Christ, a novel by Cliff Williamson

Shadows of Robyst, a novel by K. E. Maroudas

Home Within a Landscape, a novel by Alexey L. Kovalev

Motherhood, a novel by Siamak Vakili

Death, The Pharmacist, a novel by D. Ike Horst

Mystery of the Lost Years, a novel by Bobby J. Bixler

Bone Deep Bonds, a novel by B. G. Arnold

Terriers in the Jungle, a novel by Georja Umano

Into the Emerald Dream, a novel by Autumn Allen

His Name Was Ellis, a novel by Joseph Libonati

The Cup, a novel by D. P. Hardwick

The Empathy Academy, a novel by Dustin Grinnell

Tholocco's Wake, a novel by W. W. VanOverbeke

Dying to Live, a novel by Barbara Macpherson Reyelts

Looking for Lawson, a novel by Mark Kirby

ABOUT THE AUTHOR

Author J.A. Adams, PhD, is currently retired in Northern Colorado after teaching English for sixteen years at Louisiana State University. She is the author of *Pillars of Salt*.

Inspiration for her latest novel, *Bomb Cyclone*, came from Russia's annexation of Crimea from Ukraine in 2014, and addresses the effect of the resulting unrest on a Ukrainian American émigré and the beautiful spy sent by the SVR to acquire the bomb coordinates in his possession.

CPSIA information can be obtained
at www.ICGtesting.com
Printed in the USA
LVHW020429140922
728284LV00005B/145